W9-AWS-635

———————— ★ ————————

The scream rising in me couldn't squeeze through my tight throat. My stomach heaved in protest. Pressing my hand against my mouth, I backed away, unable to tear my eyes from the grisly sight. I kept backing away until I bumped into the door. I tore it open and ran outside.

I kept running until I hit the fence at the edge of the parking lot. Clutching the cool chain links with one hand, I swayed. My stomach violently rejected all I had eaten. I continued to heave long after there was nothing left to expel. When I was finally able to stop, I collapsed with my back against the fence. At first I concentrated on breathing deeply, on regaining some control over my shaking body.

When the trembling ceased, I tried to put my thoughts in order.

Galen Crawford was dead.

———————— ★ ————————

ILSA MAYR

A TIMELY ALIBI

WORLDWIDE®

TORONTO • NEW YORK • LONDON
AMSTERDAM • PARIS • SYDNEY • HAMBURG
STOCKHOLM • ATHENS • TOKYO • MILAN
MADRID • WARSAW • BUDAPEST • AUCKLAND

If you purchased this book without a cover you should be aware that this book is stolen property. It was reported as "unsold and destroyed" to the publisher, and neither the author nor the publisher has received any payment for this "stripped book."

Recycling programs
for this product may
not exist in your area.

A TIMELY ALIBI

A Worldwide Mystery/December 2010

First published by Thomas Bouregy & Co., Inc.

ISBN-13: 978-0-373-26735-4

Copyright © 2004 by Ilse Dallmayr
All rights reserved. No part of this book may be reproduced or transmitted in any form or by any means, electronic or mechanical, including photocopying, recording or by any information storage and retrieval system, without permission in writing from the publisher. For information, contact: Avalon Books, Thomas Bouregy & Co., Inc., 160 Madison Ave., New York, NY 10016 U.S.A.

This is a work of fiction. Names, characters, places and incidents are either the product of the author's imagination or are used fictitiously, and any resemblance to actual persons, living or dead, business establishments, events or locales is entirely coincidental.

® and TM are trademarks of Harlequin Enterprises Limited. Trademarks indicated with ® are registered in the United States Patent and Trademark Office, the Canadian Trade Marks Office and in other countries.

Printed in U.S.A.

This book is dedicated to my librarian friends—
mystery lovers all—who are, in alphabetical order,
as librarians love alphabetical order: Mary Lue Binning,
Helene Evans and Berneice Wilson.

ONE

Terrance Ariosto was rumored to be the richest man in Westport, Indiana.

He was arguably the stingiest man.

He was definitely the meanest.

I had helped his daughter, Annette, squeak through our algebra class in high school, and so I'd had lots of chances to observe him up close and personal. Every time I'd gone to the estate, I'd prayed that his fearsome temper outbursts and his snide, sarcastic remarks wouldn't be directed at me.

So, knowing all that, why was I sitting in his elegant study, waiting for him to get off the phone? Because he had asked for me specifically when he hired the Keller Security Agency to investigate a problem for him. Barney Keller, my uncle and boss, gave me the assignment. This was my first chance to prove myself as an apprentice investigator. I was impatient to get on with it. Ariosto must have sensed this.

Covering the mouthpiece of the phone with his hand, he mouthed, "I'll be with you in a minute."

I nodded and crossed my legs. Touching the fine wool of my skirt, I reassured myself that my suit looked professional. For what it had cost, it should. Not that I had paid the original, inflated price. Although I adore clothes, I never buy anything in the department stores lining Chicago's Miracle Mile unless it has been marked down three times. Thinking of my favorite store, I realized I hadn't been shopping in a little over a year. Not since... I jumped on the memory hard.

I moved in the chair slightly so that I could steal a quick look at the photo on the antique pedestal desk. It was a portrait of Pauline Ariosto, his fourth wife. She was probably my age, thirty. That made her a good thirty-five years younger than her husband and the same age as his only daughter, Annette. It was fortunate that none of my psychology professors had been disciples of Freud. That saved me a lot of speculation about complexes originating in Greek mythology.

Ariosto hung up the phone. He removed his wire-rimmed glasses and looked at me.

"All right. Let's get down to business, Cybil. Or shall I call you Mrs. Quindt?"

"Cybil is fine." For a man his size his voice struck me as unusually high and reedy. I don't like high voices, but that wouldn't keep me from doing my very best for him.

"I asked for you because I've heard that you are a first-rate investigator."

"Mr. Ariosto, I work for my uncle's agency, but I'm not a licensed investigator," I felt obligated to point out. "At least not yet."

He waved his hand dismissingly. "That doesn't matter. From what I hear, you get results. So, after working in my warehouse for several days, what do you have to report?"

"Your suspicions were right."

"I'm being ripped off. I knew it!"

He smashed his fist on the desktop. The photo of Pauline toppled over. He didn't bother to set it upright.

"Who the hell is stealing from me?" he demanded.

A dull, angry red color suffused his skin. I could almost hear him grinding his teeth, and I wondered uneasily if I was about to witness one of his famous temper tantrums. Bracing myself, I said, "Let's get a couple of things straight, Mr. Ariosto. I won't do anything that's illegal, and when I discover who the thieves are, I'll call the police before I call you."

A hint of a grim smile pulled at his thin lips. "Afraid I'll take them apart limb by limb?"

"Something like that."

"You're right. I'm angry enough to go after a grizzly with a stick."

To underscore his words, he cracked his knuckles. I believed him and wanted no part of this. When I made a move to stand up, he waved me down.

"Hold on. I am angry, but I'm not stupid. As much as it would pleasure me to kick…rumps, I won't risk going to jail on an assault charge."

I must have looked skeptical.

"You have my word on that."

Since he had a reputation for keeping his word, I leaned back in my seat.

Ariosto lit a fat cigar, not bothering to ask me if I minded the smoke. *I* did, but since I was in his house and he was an important client, I kept my mouth shut.

"Well, I've known for some time that profits at the Tri State Warehouses were down, but I blamed it on the recession we'd been having. When things didn't perk up but got worse this summer, I knew something was fishy. How bad is it?"

I glanced at the figures in my small notebook. "I estimate you're losing about twenty thousand dollars worth of goods a month. Of course, that's only an educated guess."

For a second he sat as if struck by lightning. Then a stream of expletives spewed from his mouth that would have gladdened the heart of a drunken sailor. After he paused for breath, he demanded, "Who's stealing me blind?"

"Pilfering on this scale must involve an organized theft ring."

"Does that make discovering the thieves more difficult?" he asked.

"No. It would be harder, if not impossible, to catch the random individual sneaking out a pound of butter or a couple of steaks."

Ariosto nodded. "We expect some petty pilfering. That's built into the nature of the business. But not twenty thousand dollars worth. You must have some idea who's doing it."

"Yes, but we want the man or the men who organized the operation, who contacted the places that receive the extra cases of caviar, veal and lobster. We need proof of who gets the payoff."

"Exactly. I want to nail their thieving hides to the warehouse doors." He puffed forcefully on his cigar. "It's going to be hard to find out who these men are," he muttered.

"Not necessarily. An organized group has to meet occasionally to make plans and divvy up the money.

That's how we'll nab them. Uncle Barney says that it's the extra income that gets people caught. If they would salt the money away, they'd be free and clear but most of them don't. They buy things. It's not difficult to spot someone living above their legitimate income."

"Where will you start? How will you do it?" He held up his hand. "No, don't tell me. Just do it. Bring me proof and report to me here at the house. I can't be sure who's in on this at my office. Seems I can't trust anybody."

Since the food distribution warehouse was only one of his many business ventures, I doubted that his entire staff was involved but didn't say so. We shook hands, and I left.

On the portico I almost collided with Pauline Ariosto rushing into the house. Judging by her red, puffy eyes, she had been crying. Life on top of the hill was apparently not any more Edenic than it was in the valley where the rest of us lived.

My UNCLE'S AGENCY takes up the second floor of a building whose designer had obviously liked Renaissance architecture. This preference was especially apparent in the frieze below the roof and in the treatment of doors and windows. I love the architect's disregard for the purely functional.

Lynn, which is the Americanization of her Vietnamese name she insists on using, was arguing with Glenn, one of the investigators, when I entered the office.

"No receipt, no reimbursement. You know that," the efficient office manager said coolly.

"I already explained it to you. I didn't have time to

get the receipt. The subject I was following had already paid the toll and was speeding toward Chicago."

"Too bad. Next time follow more closely."

Discussion closed, Lynn swiveled her chair to face the computer. Moments later the furious tapping of the keys filled the room.

I looked at Glenn with sympathy. The only way he would get reimbursed was to appeal directly to my uncle. Barney Keller is the one person for whom Lynn will break the elaborate set of rules and procedures she has set up for running the office. I'm not sure, but I think my uncle met Lynn in Vietnam during the war. Sometimes I wonder if they were, or still are, lovers. If so, they are extremely discreet.

Like a penitent, I stood in front of Lynn waiting for her to acknowledge my presence. Sometimes that takes several minutes. When she finally raised those beautiful, black, almond-shaped eyes, I asked, "Is my uncle in?"

"Yes."

"May I see him?"

"I'll announce you."

She always does that, even if his door is wide open.

After murmuring into the phone, she said, "He will see you."

"Thank you," I said, playing along with her formal ritual.

My uncle waved me to his visitor's chair. "So, what did Ariosto say?"

I reported my meeting as succinctly as I could. Barney Keller retired from the army after thirty years to open this agency. He insists on brevity and clarity.

"We are to contact him only at his home," I said in conclusion.

Barney raised an eyebrow. "His house?"

"Yes. He insists on absolute secrecy. He wants only the three of us to know about this. I suspect he's at least as embarrassed as he's furious that someone is ripping him off."

"Yeah. He's the kind of man who can't stand anyone betraying him in any way. His ego won't stand for it."

"I told him I'd continue working at Tri State until I knew the identity of the organizers and had solid proof."

Barney frowned. "I don't like you doing undercover work. If anyone suspects anything, you could be in danger."

"Nobody will suspect me of being anything but an employee. I'm careful and discreet. You know I have the kind of face that inspires people to confide in me without me having to do more than drop a hint or two."

"That's what makes you a natural investigator. But be careful anyway. Your grandmother would skin me alive if anything happened to you. If there's even a hint of danger, you get out. Agreed?"

"Agreed." I rose to my feet.

"Have you seen Mother yet?"

"She's here? Oma's here?"

"Upstairs, waiting in your office. Didn't Lynn tell you?"

She hadn't. If she thinks a message is of a personal nature she often holds it until the end of business hours. I clamped my teeth together to keep from saying anything disparaging about Lynn. However much she irritates me, I keep quiet for Uncle Barney's sake. Outside my immediate family, he's my favorite relative. Always has been.

"If it's okay, I'll go see Oma."

Barney smiled and nodded.

Although I call my grandmother Oma, which is the Austrian equivalent of granny, in my mind I refer to Maximilianne by her shortened first name, Maxi. Like her name, there's something regal about her. Perhaps it's the way she carries herself, or the set of the white-haired head. She's also tough. She had to be to leave her native Austria in 1938 with the prominent Jewish family for whom she worked as an assistant nanny. At age fifteen she'd kissed her mother and her siblings goodbye, not knowing when or if she would see them again.

I paused in the doorway to look at Maxi. Deeply engrossed in one of the paperbacks she always carried with her, she wasn't aware that I studied her with anxious eyes, looking for, and fearing to find, signs of ill health and decline. I released the breath I'd been holding. She looked just fine, her white hair coiled into an elegant twist, one of her cameo brooches pinned to the lapel of her lavender jacket. That told me that her hands hadn't hurt too much from the arthritis that plagued her from time to time.

"Hi, Oma."

Maxi smiled even before she looked up from her book and that sweet smile enfolded me with warmth like heated flannel sheets on a bitter cold winter night.

"There you are, *Schatzi*. Barney told me you went to meet with a client."

I nodded. "Why didn't you let me know you were

coming into town? I might have been able to arrange for us to go to lunch."

"I will next time. I keep forgetting that you're a working woman again. Do you still like working for Barney?"

Scooting my chair from behind the metal desk, I sat down facing her. "I still like working as an investigator. Maybe even more now that I know what I'm doing. Uncle Barney's been training me. It's exciting. The days fly by where before they didn't seem to want to end. I'll always remember that you and Uncle Barney did this for me." I reached for Maxi's hand and held it against my cheek. She smoothed my hair with her other hand. "Thank you again, Oma."

"You're welcome," she murmured. "We couldn't stand by any longer and watch you grow paler and more withdrawn each day. So Barney hit on the idea of hiring you. He always claimed you were the brightest of my grandchildren. And you know what? He's right. What is that American saying? It takes one to know one?"

I nodded.

"Of my six children Barney's also the one with the kindest heart and that makes him a good man." Maxi stroked my hair one more time. "How about some tea? You still have that hot pot in your file cabinet?"

"Yes. I'll get the water from the cooler in the hall."

When I returned, she had set out cups, sugar, and napkins. I set the pot on top of the cabinet and plugged it in. "What brought you into town today?"

"The anniversary. The same thing that drove you to the cemetery first thing this morning."

I must have looked surprised because Maxi felt it necessary to explain.

"Luke told me. He saw you at the cemetery. Though I would have known that the yellow roses were from you."

I nodded. "Yellow was Ryan's favorite color. It suited him, don't you think? He was such a sunny, even-tempered child." My voice broke. The pain in my throat from suppressed tears was excruciating. I busied myself with the box of tea bags, opening it, closing it, repeating the gesture until I could speak again.

"I went at six this morning. It seemed right. Ryan always woke up at that time, full of energy, ready to face all the exciting discoveries a new day would bring." Of the many things my sweet little boy would never experience were his fourth birthday, the new tricycle we were planning to give him, his first day in preschool, camping out that summer in Oma's meadow... I bit my lower lip hard, welcoming the physical pain.

After a while I asked, "You said you saw my husband. How is Luke?"

"He seemed okay. He has his work. I suspect he leaves the hospital only long enough to sleep and change clothes."

"Then why doesn't he understand that working is important to me, too?" I poured the boiling water over the tea bags. "He hates my working here."

"He's afraid. He's lost a son. He can't bear the thought of losing his wife, too," Maxi said softly.

"I understand that, but it's so illogical. The chance of me being killed in a car crash or an accident in the home are so much greater than anything happening to me on the job. Luke wants us to be like we were before Ryan's death and that's impossible. We're not the same people now we were then. Why can't he accept that?"

"He will, just as he will come to terms with your work. He has to. It's kept you from—"

"Oma, you can say it: from having a nervous breakdown. From going off the deep end." I poured the tea. We sipped it silently, each of us pursuing our own thoughts. After a while I heard Maxi sigh.

"Any chance of your moving back in with Luke?" she asked.

"Not any time soon. I need to be on my own. I can't live in a house that holds all those memories."

"That's why you bought and moved into that fixer-upper's dream. Or nightmare, depending on how you look at that house. I think I understand," Maxi said.

"Well, that's more than Luke does."

"I repeat, give him time, *Schatzi*."

"I'm sorry I'm such a wet blanket today."

"You're never that." Changing subjects, she said, with a sigh, "I'm having dinner with your mother and her husband tonight."

"Ah."

"I'm ashamed to admit this, but I would rather finish my book than listen to Justin Merriweather pontificate about banking and investments. The only thing that will make the evening bearable is the excellent food. Your mother has always managed to hire first rate cooks."

We smiled at each other in perfect understanding.

"What are you reading?"

"Actually, I'm rereading. One of Jane Austen's. I wish she had written more books."

"There *are* some good modern writers," I said.

"I know, and I've tried them, but somehow I always return to Jane." Maxi shrugged, smiling apologetically. She stuffed her book into the seemingly bottomless knitting bag she uses for her everyday purse.

We hugged each other before I walked her to the door of the agency.

After Maxi's visit I sat at my desk, staring out the window, remembering, brooding. Then I forced myself back to the task of trying to figure out a way to get proof of the pilfering.

THE NEXT MORNING I ran a little late and hurried into the warehouse just as the bell rang, announcing the beginning of the shift.

"Hey, Elsie Timms!"

Belatedly I remembered that Elsie Timms was the alias I was using at Tri State. I stopped and turned. The foreman crooked a finger, signaling me to join him where he stood, clipboard in hand.

"I'm assigning you to work permanently with Wilma's team."

"Yes, Mr. Walters," I said.

"My, my. Ain't you the polite one. Call me Subby."

Not if I could help it. He had a dirty, leering grin that made my skin crawl.

"You get along with Wilma, don't you? She's the one in the wheelchair."

I nodded. How could I not remember Wilma? I hadn't expected a physically handicapped person to work in a warehouse. Rail-thin and fragile-looking, Wilma zoomed around in her mechanized chair as if she were in training for the Indy 500.

On cue, she sped toward us, braking on a dime in front of Subby. He jumped back.

"Jesus, Wilma, watch out. You're dangerous in that thing."

She merely grinned, looking like a pixie.

"If you have any questions or complaints about anything, I'm the man who'll take care of you." Subby hitched up his pants in that swaggering, typically male gesture before he turned and headed toward the back of the warehouse.

"Don't worry about him," Wilma said. "He's mostly hot air." She plucked an order form from the pile in her lap and handed it to me. "Pick up the items and group them on the conveyer. Most of them are arranged alphabetically."

I KEPT AN EAGLE EYE on the orders I filled, but nothing out of the ordinary happened during the next two days. Or I didn't see it. On the third, I paused to watch one of my orders being loaded onto the truck. I could have sworn that the invoice called for only one carton of coffee, not four. I retrieved and examined the carbon copy of the order.

"Something wrong?" Latoya asked.

She was part of Wilma's team. "Just double checking," I said.

"Don't," she warned in a low tone. "Not if you want to keep your job."

Wilma joined us.

"Even if I think something extra's been added to the order?"

She shrugged. "That's up to you. A guy got fired for mentioning that. Me, I got three kids to support."

"What was the guy's name who got fired?"

Latoya suddenly spotted something she had to do and hurried off.

"Hiram Greene," Wilma said and moved away before I could ask her anything else. While I worked on my next order, I kept wondering how to get the women to talk about what they obviously suspected.

When the lunch whistle blew, I went to my car to fetch the peanut butter sandwich I'd left there deliberately so that I could use my cell phone to report to Uncle Barney. I told him about Hiram Greene. He promised to run a check on the man and get his story. Anticipating that I might have to stay at the warehouse after everyone had left, I moved my rented car out of Tri State's lot and parked it down the block.

My arms and back hurt from all that lifting. I was glad of the chance to sit down in the lunch room, even though the mismatched chairs were hard and the room ugly and uncomfortable.

"The women sit together," Latoya said. "The men prefer to sit by themselves so they can lie and brag without being called on their exaggerations. Tell you the truth, I'd just as soon not have to listen to all that b.s." She rolled her expressive black eyes.

"Not all the women sit together," I said, nodding toward a redhead who had joined the men. "Is that her husband next to her?"

Latoya snorted.

"Cathy's husband doesn't work here anymore," Wilma said.

I saw that Wilma looked pale, almost stricken and sensed a sudden tension around the table.

"Good thing Tom Carnes quit. We'd have nothing but brawls because of her flirting," Latoya said.

A couple of the women snickered. I thought her statement had been an attempt to break the tense silence. What had happened at Tri State when Cathy's husband had worked here?

By the end of the shift, I didn't see any noticeable changes in the orders on the conveyor belts. Most of the pilfered items had to be added after hours. That made sense.

I clocked out, and pretending I'd left something in the lunch room, I walked back in that direction. On the way I angled toward the conveyor belt nearest the wall. There I ducked behind the boxes I had stacked earlier so that they formed a crude hiding place from where I could watch the conveyors.

The warehouse grew silent. The minutes crept by like somnolent snails. My stomach growled with hunger. I was hot, and my neck was going to have a painful crick in it from holding my head at the unnatural angle necessary to peek through a crack in the wall of boxes.

Hearing footsteps, I froze, hardly daring to breathe. In my haste to build the hideout, I hadn't calculated the angle of my vision. All I could see of the thief were his jean-clad legs and feet. Fortunately he wore somewhat unusual shoes: black lace-up work shoes with metal caps over the toes.

It took him forever to add the pilfered goods to the piles on the dock. Or so it seemed to me in my anxiety-ridden frame of mind. If he discovered me, I had no idea what explanation I could offer that had even a slight chance of being believable. My best bet would be to play an irrational, hysterical woman. I could do that.

When I heard the dock doors being closed and the lights went out, I forced myself to count to one hundred before I flicked on my pencil flashlight. By its meager beam I made my way to the ladies' room where I climbed out through the window.

DURING OUR COFFEE BREAK the next morning, I sat beside Wilma. In a low voice I asked her, "Do you know who wears metal-tipped, black work boots?"

She looked at me for a moment before she answered. "Subby has a pair."

That made sense. As the foreman of the warehouse, it would be hard for him not to be involved.

"Why do you want to know about Subby's special work boots? There's something going on around here, isn't there?"

"What makes you think that, Wilma?"

"I don't know."

"But you have some idea," I suggested.

She seemed to be debating with herself. Finally she said, "There have been times when I thought an order was lots bigger than it should have been. Is that what you think, too?"

I nodded.

"Who are you? A cop?"

"No."

"The FBI?"

"No."

"Can I help?"

Her voice was filled with youthful enthusiasm and sounded as though she thought this might be fun. I had to disabuse her of that notion. "No, Wilma. Forget that I asked you anything."

"Why? Because I'm a cripple in a wheelchair?"

"No, because I don't want you to lose your job just because I'm incurably nosy." I shrugged. "My grandma is always quoting the old saying to me about curiosity killing the cat." I excused myself and went to the ladies' room.

There I took a pair of opera glasses and a camera from my shoulder bag. Then I opened the window, stood back, and focused the opera glasses on the truck backed up to the dock. I wrote down every item that was loaded. I intended to compare my inventory to the official invoice. Remembering that Uncle Barney is a firm believer in the saying that a picture is worth a thousand words, I took several photos of the loading process and the license plate of the truck.

Now all I had to do was find out the destination of the trucks. Since lunch wasn't over yet, the warehouse was deserted. I'd seen where Subby had placed his clipboard with the invoices. Quickly I located the right invoice and photographed it. The truck with the added items went to the Neapolitan Restaurant and then to St. Anne's Retirement Home.

I was on the board of Eldercare, a watchdog agency for the elderly. If the home was in on this scheme, we hadn't been very good watchdogs.

I headed toward my place on the assembly line just as the whistle blew, announcing the end of lunch.

AFTER WORK I STOPPED at the hardware store and picked up some nails, paint stripper, and sandpaper. By the time I stepped on my front porch, it was getting dark. When I caught a movement in my peripheral vision, I let out a startled yelp. Then I recognized my husband's lean runner's body.

"Luke! You scared me half to death."

"You should be scared. This is not the safest neighborhood. Why didn't you at least leave the porch light on?" he demanded.

Because it didn't work. Many things in my old Victorian house didn't work. I didn't tell him that. He hadn't been inside the house yet, so I knew he would find lots to criticize. I didn't need to give him additional ammunition. Unlocking the front door, I motioned for him to enter. I flipped the light switch.

"That's some chandelier," he said. "And it's in perfect condition. Was it like that?"

"No. Fortunately, the one in the upstairs hall had the same crystal teardrops so I combined the two to make one chandelier."

Luke glanced around curiously.

I had stripped half the paint off from the banister, so it looked truly hideous. The floor of the foyer was lined with newspapers to protect the wood underneath. I followed his glance as he assessed the living room where the wallpaper had been removed down to the dingy walls.

"There's lots of work to be done yet," I said defensively.

"Did you come to help?" He turned and gave me one of his penetrating stares. "I guess you didn't, so what can I do for you?"

"How long is this farce going to go on?"

"If you're talking about my life, I don't consider it a farce."

"Not your life, Cybil. This house. It'll take years to whip it into shape. That or tons of money which I know you don't have. If you needed a place of your own, why not rent an apartment? Or get a nice, new condominium?"

I set my bag down. "Something about this house called out to me. It needed rescuing." Like me, but I didn't say that. "I can't explain it."

"Maxi said you were on a new assignment. In a warehouse?"

"Yes."

Luke ran his hand through his dark hair, a gesture of frustration I knew well. I could see him struggle for composure before he spoke.

"Jesus, Cybil, I don't understand you. You're a first-class social worker and school guidance counselor. You're on the boards of several important committees that help kids and old people. If you want to work, why not in your own field?"

"I'm not up to that emotionally."

"But you are up to working in a warehouse."

Luke was more upset about this than I had first assumed. "What's really bothering you? Are you embarrassed? Is it a disgrace for a doctor's wife to work in a warehouse? Don't worry. I used an alias." His eyes narrowed dangerously.

"You know me better than that. I wish to God you'd never started with this investigation stuff."

"Now we're getting at the truth. You were all for it in the beginning. What's changed?"

"When your uncle offered you a job, I thought it was a good idea. It got you out of the house. For the first time since Ryan's death, you showed an interest in something. But I didn't anticipate you'd actually go out and personally investigate criminal activities. I thought your uncle would keep you busy with some office work—"

"Ah, you thought I'd be playing at the job. Now it's my turn to say 'you should know me better than that'. I don't do things halfway."

"How long are you planning to work as an investigator?"

"I hadn't thought about it, but now that you mention it, I have no intention of quitting. I like the work and oddly enough, I'm quite good at it." We looked at each other, neither of us prepared to back down. "What bothers you about my job?"

"It's potentially dangerous. Don't tell me that it isn't because I know better. I work in the ER and I see the victims of violence daily. Don't tell me that men are going to let you snoop into their business without getting furious or maybe even physical. I don't want you hurt. Is that so difficult to understand?"

"No," I admitted, feeling guilty and defensive. Still, I couldn't back down. We stood facing each other, much farther apart than the few feet between us.

"If the tables were turned, wouldn't you worry about me?"

He had me there and he knew it. "Damn it, Luke. I

hate it when you're so infuriatingly logical and right."
I moved my head. Pain shot through my neck. I must
have grimaced because Luke noticed.

"What's wrong?" Luke touched my neck, my shoulders. "You're as stiff as a side of frozen beef. Come, lie
down."

I let him lead me to the couch in the living room and
lay down on it, face down. Luke massaged my neck
and my shoulders. I could feel the stiffness ease. We
hadn't resolved our disagreement about my work or the
house, but I was beginning to feel too relaxed to pursue
the subject. I don't know precisely when Luke's touch
changed, but it did.

"Turn over," he murmured after a while, his mouth
tender against my nape.

The telephone rang before I could comply with his
seductive request.

Luke muttered something and got up to answer it. A
moment later he said, "It's for you. Barney."

My uncle didn't waste words on small talk.

"The woman you mentioned? Wilma Johnson? I just
heard a police report. She's dead."

TWO

I SAT DOWN HEAVILY in the nearest chair. My mind was numb as I listened to my uncle relate the scanty bits of news he had. According to Sam Keller, my cousin on the Westport police force, Wilma's wheelchair plunged down a flight of stairs in her apartment building. The medical examiner pronounced her dead at the scene. My cousin thought it was an accident.

"That's hard to believe," I said more to myself than to Uncle Barney.

"Why?"

"Because Wilma maneuvered that wheelchair the way the Unsers drive race cars."

"Accidents do happen."

The more I thought about it the less I believed it was an accident. "The way she guided those wheels through the narrow aisles in the warehouse and up and down the loading ramps…no, it doesn't make sense for her to careen down an ordinary flight of stairs."

"If it wasn't an accident, can you think of any reason why someone would push her?"

Briefly I told Uncle Barney about my conversation with Wilma. Feeling guilt nibble at my conscience, I said, justifying myself, "I didn't ask her to help me. I pretended to be casually nosy."

"Do you think she bought your explanation?"

My mouth was dry. I had trouble speaking. "I thought so, but she wasn't dumb. She probably suspected that something was wrong in that warehouse. I'd feel better if I knew where Subby Walters was at the time of her death."

"So would I." He was quiet for a moment. "We're going to have to tell the police about our investigation. I'll call Ariosto about it."

"He isn't going to like that."

"We have no choice but to involve the cops if someone helped Wilma down those steps."

I agreed with him.

"Uncle Barney, did you ever get a hold of Hiram Greene? The guy who was fired from Tri State for asking questions?"

"I met him at the bar of his choice. At first he didn't want to talk, but after a couple of Coronas, he opened up. Like you, he noticed that some orders got considerably larger by the time they reached the truck."

"Did he mention any specific places?"

"Joe's Steak Emporium. Miami Bar and Grill. The Coterie. The Neapolitan, and Mom's."

"Isn't Mom's a diner?"

"It is. Open twenty-four hours a day. Mom's probably didn't get any lobster or veal, but can you imagine how many burgers and hot dogs they serve?"

"Did he mention to whom he told his suspicions?" I asked.

"Subby Walters, the foreman, and Lyle Novak, the supervisor of the warehouses."

"What did they say?"

"They told him he better find another job, and if he

mentioned this to anyone else, he wouldn't get a recommendation. He'd never work in Westport again," Barney said.

"And he believed them."

"He did."

"I think someone higher up in the company hierarchy has to be involved as well. Someone in accounting."

"I agree," Barney said. "You be careful. When this much money is involved, people get ruthless. I've seen it happen time and time again. And keep me posted."

"I will, Uncle Barney." I hung up, unable to believe that Wilma was dead. Had she checked some of the invoices and been caught snooping?

"Are you going to be all right, staying here by yourself?" Luke asked.

For a second I was tempted to ask him to stay, to hold me, but that would be a mistake. We hadn't resolved any of our differences.

"I'll be okay," I said, trying to sound convincing.

Luke touched my face briefly and walked out the door. I'm not sure he believed me, but obviously he thought it was best that he left.

For the next hour I exercised on my floor mat. The slow hatha yoga postures require intense concentration. Ordinarily I can dismiss everything from my mind, focusing on the stretches, on the particular muscles involved, on proper breathing, but not tonight. Wilma's young face with the old, old eyes kept intruding, kept making me wonder if my investigation had caused her to become curious and say something to the wrong person.

Guilt doesn't promote sleep, so after a while I

showered. Wrapped in the quilt Luke's grandmother had pieced for me, I curled up on the living room sofa to read. Toward morning I must have fallen asleep for several hours because at six I woke up, feeling groggy and stiff.

WHEN I ARRIVED AT THE warehouse people stood in groups, somber-faced, discussing Wilma's death. Suddenly the p.a. system crackled and a man's voice, one of the top executives, I suspected, informed us of her loss, adding the name of the funeral home and the date of the viewing.

Subdued, Latoya and I set to work. Even though I hadn't known Wilma well, I missed her. The place wasn't the same without her zipping around in her motorized chair.

During our morning break, Subby Walters joined us. "You ladies are on your own today. Farrell promised to hire someone to replace Wilma as soon as possible. Until then, do the best you can."

He didn't look shocked by the tragedy or especially affected, I thought, but that wasn't necessarily a sign of guilt. He could be one of those men who pride themselves on never showing their deeper emotions.

"I like the way he offered to help us, don't you?" Latoya frowned at Subby's broad, retreating back.

Pouring coffee into the cup of my thermos bottle, I debated briefly with myself before I decided to question Latoya. "How did Wilma end up in a wheelchair?"

Latoya blew on her coffee to cool it. "Car accident last December. During the first major snowstorm we had. Remember it?"

I nodded. The first storm of the season usually causes lots of fender benders because people have forgotten how to drive on snow and ice.

"It was a miracle that either one of them survived," she added.

"Did Wilma drive?"

"Yeah. Tri State has a women's bowling team. Wilma and Mae Carnes, Cathy's mother-in-law, always rode together. We bowled that night. When we started it was just drizzling a little, but three hours later five inches of snow had fallen on top of the icy streets. It was real bad. Wilma's car hit a patch of ice and went over the embankment on the bypass. Mae was badly hurt, too. She never came back to work. I guess she qualified for early retirement or disability or something. And then a couple of weeks ago she passed away."

A bowling alley. I have been in one maybe three times in my life but I remember that most of them serve beer. Had Wilma been drinking? As if she read my mind, Latoya continued.

"We won that night, so we had a few beers to celebrate, but nobody was drunk."

"Did Wilma just move into the building where she fell down the stairs?"

"No. She's lived there since June when she returned to work. What are you getting at?"

"I thought if it were a new place it might explain why someone who handled a wheelchair as expertly as she did would plunge down the steps."

Latoya looked at me, her face as expressionless as an Ashanti mask. She drank some coffee before she spoke.

"I wondered about that, too. She could pilot that thing in her sleep."

"Any ideas? Explanations?"

She shook her head, setting her dreadlocks in motion. "Wilma didn't drink anymore, and she didn't do drugs."

"Did you know her well?"

"Yeah. Sometimes she'd come to my place for a meal or to play cards. Once in a while she'd watch my kids so I could go out. And as I said, we bowled together."

"Did she live alone?"

Latoya nodded. "Her momma remarried. Wilma didn't want to be in the way. That's what she said, but I suspect she didn't much like her new stepdaddy, so when she was ready to come back to work, she moved into an apartment. She was proud of her place. Fixed it up nice."

Could Wilma's dislike of her stepfather have escalated into domestic violence? Since they didn't live together, I doubted it. "Did she have a boyfriend?"

"Not since the accident."

"Did she have trouble with anyone here at the warehouse?"

"Not that I know of."

We were eliminating possible suspects right and left. All except Walters and his fellow thieves. "Did she say anything to you about the pilfering here?"

Latoya finished her coffee in one long pull and screwed the top back onto her thermos in a decisive motion. "No, she didn't, and I ain't saying nothing either." With that she went back to work.

I MET UNCLE BARNEY at the Ariosto estate. Our meeting with Ariosto was shorter than the time it took to drive to his house. The butler, Brazier, led us into the study. Ariosto agreed somewhat sourly that we should tell the police about our investigation if it became absolutely necessary.

Having settled that, Ariosto demanded, "What have you found out so far?"

"After comparing the official invoice with what actually went on the truck, I think our original estimate of losses might be too conservative. Even though this is only one delivery, I don't see what would keep the thieves from being less generous with the other orders," I told him.

"Where did this shipment go to?"

"The Neapolitan restaurant."

"God dammit," Ariosto yelled. "That son of a gun, Guiseppe. I bailed him out three years ago when his restaurant was going under. Now he's ripping me off. That's gratitude for you."

"He might not know anything about it. His chef could be buying the stolen goods and pocketing the profit," I said, trying to placate Ariosto's fury. One look at his thin-lipped mouth and his glittering eyes and I shut up. He was obviously fighting to control his anger.

"I want his ass on a platter, and I want it fast. Are you documenting this?" he demanded.

"Yes," I said, surreptitiously crossing my fingers. Those photographs had better turn out okay.

Ariosto dismissed us, anger clearly boiling in him.

"I hope he doesn't do anything foolish to Guiseppe," I said to Barney.

"If he does, there's nothing we can do about it."

We stopped at my car.

"Where did you get this?" Barney asked, looking at the beige Ford Escort.

"I rented it. I couldn't very well apply for a job in a warehouse driving my Volvo." Barney nodded his approval. I trusted he would put in a good word for me when I presented the rental charge to Lynn.

"When will you be ready for a surveillance team?" he asked.

"Soon. I haven't yet identified all the truck drivers who are part of the operation."

"Are you going home now?"

"No. I want to take a look at Wilma's building. I need to check out those stairs."

"Good idea. I'll follow you."

Wilma's apartment, located on the third floor of a remodeled factory, featured ramps and an elevator with a bench. Inside, the halls were extra wide to accommodate wheelchairs. Wilma's corner apartment was located a good distance from the elevator and the stairs.

While we were studying the layout, my cousin, Lieutenant Sam Keller, came out of Wilma's apartment. Like most of the Keller men, Sam is tall, fair-haired, blue-eyed. Unfortunately, he has also inherited the family tendency toward baldness. At thirty-five his hairline has receded noticeably.

"What are you two doing here?" Sam asked. He opened a flip-top box, pulled out a cigarette and lit it with a disposable lighter.

"We wanted to take a look at the stairs," Barney explained. "Are you officially calling it an accident?"

"There's nothing to indicate that it was anything else. The brakes on the wheelchair were off, and no one saw or heard anything out of the ordinary."

"Why would Wilma have gone near the stairs at all?" I asked Sam. "Even if she'd been waiting at the elevator, she would have been too far from the stairs to have tumbled down accidentally."

"She could have been on her way to visit someone down that end of the hall. Everybody said she was friendly and sociable. Maybe she waited for someone at the top of the stairs," Sam answered.

"That still doesn't explain how she fell down," I insisted.

"Maybe she miscalculated. Maybe she pushed the wrong button on the chair. Maybe she got dizzy. Hell, Cybil, there could be a dozen reasons."

I shook my head emphatically.

"Lord, you're still as stubborn as you always were," he said.

"I'm not stubborn per se, but when I'm convinced I'm right about something, I don't back down easily," I corrected him.

"I remember when we were kids," Sam said with a rueful expression, "how you used to dig in your heels like a little mule to get your way, but it's not going to work this time. There's not a single solid shred of evidence that it was anything but an accident."

Ignoring my cousin's incorrect and unfair interpretation of my character, I asked, "Uncle Barney, do you want to tell Sam or should I?"

Barney filled him in on the pilfering at Tri State.

"Is Ariosto going to call us in on that?" Sam asked.

"Not yet."

"Then there's nothing I can do."

Sam lifted his hand to forestall my objections.

"Give me proof of foul play or probable cause or anything at all, and I'll actively pursue the case. Nice to have seen you again, Cybil. Let's have lunch sometime. Uncle Barney."

With a casual wave of his hand Sam left us. Silently we watched him take the stairs down, two at a time.

"Sam's right, you know. We have nothing but your suspicions," Barney said.

"Not yet, we don't." I punched the down button with more force than necessary. Moments later the elevator doors opened. Downstairs we met an old woman struggling with two grocery bags.

"Let us help you, ma'am," Barney offered.

He took one bag, and I the other.

"Well, bless you," she said, breathing hard. "I live on the second floor, right by the stairs."

Uncle Barney and I exchanged a look. As casually as I could, I asked, "Isn't that where Wilma Johnson had her accident?"

"Yes. Terrible thing, what happened to that nice young woman." She made a disapproving clucking noise. "I found her, you know," she confided, somewhat self-importantly.

"How awful for you," I murmured.

"I thought my heart was going to give out right then and there. I have a bad ticker, you know," she said, pressing her right hand against her thin chest. The gesture reminded me of Maxi who suffers from angina, and I felt again the stab of worry surge through me.

The elevator stopped on the second floor. We followed her down the hall. "Tell us what happened," I suggested. She didn't need much encouragement. I suspected it wasn't macabre eagerness that prompted her to talk, but loneliness. I made a promise to myself that I would come back to visit her.

"I was sitting by the kitchen window, peeling apples for a pie I was planning to bake for the church supper when I heard an awful racket in the hall. This is usually such a quiet place what with most of us being old, so naturally I went to see what happened."

She paused at her apartment door, rummaging through her black plastic handbag for the key. The cardboard name plate above the doorbell identified her as Ferne Lauder in spidery handwriting. Preceding us into the apartment, she continued.

"The first thing I saw was the wheelchair. It was upside down with the wheels still spinning. I knew right then that something dreadful must have happened. I looked to my left and saw Wilma at the bottom of the stairs, crumpled up like a rag doll. I called her name, but she didn't answer, so I rushed to the telephone and called the manager. She phoned the ambulance and the police right away, but it was too late."

"Did you see anyone in the hall? Or at the top of the stairs?" I asked.

"No. Not right away. Later other tenants came out to see what was happening."

We carried the groceries into the surprisingly roomy kitchen. The table stood in front of a large window overlooking the street where several cars were parked. That gave me an idea. "Mrs. Lauder, did you look out the window while you peeled the apples?"

"Sure. Peeling doesn't take much concentration."

"Did you notice cars parked on the street that aren't usually seen in this neighborhood?"

She wrinkled her forehead in thought. "Like what kind?" she asked after several seconds.

"Oh, I don't know. Something sporty or expensive."

She shook her head. "My grandson drives a sporty-looking car. A Trans Am. I didn't see anything like that out there."

"How about a black, four-door Cadillac?"

She shook her head. "We don't see big, expensive cars like that in this neighborhood." She thought for a moment. "You know, there was a red jeep parked catty-corner across the street that I don't remember seeing there before."

"Well, we'd better go and let you put your groceries away," I said.

"If you think of anything, Mrs. Lauder, please give us a call. Here's my card," Barney said.

"Are you with the police?" Ferne asked.

"No. I'm a private investigator." Barney showed her his I.D.

I envied him that I.D. Not that it was so difficult to get one. I knew it wasn't because I had inquired. What kept me from actively pursuing my own license was that I knew Luke would go through the roof if I became a full-fledged P.I. Still, sometime in the future....

"My, my, just like on television," Ferne said, impressed, looking at the card. "Well, thanks for helping me with the groceries. Can I offer you a beer or something?"

That took me back a bit. I hadn't expected the fragile-looking, white-haired woman wearing a lace collar with a string of pearls to keep beer in her refrigerator. She looked like the perfect ad for a fancy tea commercial. Darjeeling or maybe my favorite, Earl Grey.

"No, thank you," Barney said.

"Maybe some other time. Drop in if you're in the neighborhood," Ferne said, walking us to her door. She smiled at us until the elevator doors closed.

"The cars you asked about belong to Walters and Novak?" Barney asked.

"Yes. Of course, the car could have been parked farther down the street or even in the next block."

"True. And the murderer, if there is one, had a chance to get away unseen. Did you catch that?"

I nodded. "When Ferne went back into her apartment to phone the manager." Uncle Barney looked at me approvingly. That cheered me for about five seconds. Then I remembered our discouraging situation. "Do you realize the murderer may go free? What with the police insisting it's an accident and us not having any evidence to the contrary."

"No, we don't have any evidence yet. But we do know people who have a motive. If this is really murder. It could be a freak accident. Don't dismiss that possibility completely," he cautioned.

On that note, we parted—Barney to go to the office and I to go home and get ready for a dinner benefiting Eldercare. Putting off dressing as long as I could, I looked through the mail, walked through each room downstairs to water the plants facing the east windows, and read the newspaper.

Finally, I could procrastinate no longer. If I had a choice, I would rather come down with a good case of poison ivy than attend one of these functions. Since I didn't sprout an itchy rash, I took a bath, applied makeup a little more heavily than I ordinarily do, and slipped into my electric blue silk dress.

I added the string of fine pearls Luke had given me for our third wedding anniversary. He thinks of me as the pearl type, but I don't. My mother, on the other hand, is. Pearls complement the shimmer of her golden blond hair and the sparkle of her clear, sky-blue eyes. But then, being a truly beautiful woman, everything looks good on her.

Looking at myself in the mirror, I noticed again that I bear no resemblance to Elizabeth Keller Kruger Diver Merriweather, my much-married mother. When I was little, I used to think that I was a changeling until I saw myself in profile. At thirteen a straight nose offers small comfort.

Maxi tried to console me by saying that I had intelligence and character, qualities more valuable in the long run than golden hair. That was even less comforting. I couldn't think of a single boy in junior high who even noticed those qualities, much less found them attractive. Come to think of it, I haven't met too many mature men who prefer them to a sexy body and a flawless face.

ON THURSDAYS restaurants receive their weekend deliveries. Not surprisingly, the orders for each of the eateries mentioned by Hiram were padded with unbilled items.

I documented these with my camera. I even got a shot of Subby carrying a carton of olive oil, but I suspect a court won't consider this admissible evidence. What it will do, I hope, is soften him up for a confession when he is confronted with the photo.

So far I had identified eight truck drivers as part of the local operation. What I didn't have yet was the name of the top executive participating in the thefts and the individuals buying the pilfered goods.

After work I went home long enough to boil a handful of penne, heat the frozen marinara sauce, fix a salad, and eat my dinner while watching the evening news.

Then for the second time that day I drove to the Tri State Warehouses. Dressed in black slacks and a black pullover, my longish hair hidden under a black knit cap, I matched the darkness. I felt like a second-story jewel thief. On cue, my uncle's Oldsmobile and Glenn Brown's Toyota pulled up beside me.

Uncle Barney divided the tasks among us. While he unlocked the trucks with a skeleton key, I placed a bug under the dash, reciting "Mary had a little lamb" to test Glenn's receiver. The whole procedure went off like a perfectly executed top-level military operation. We were out of the parking lot in fourteen minutes.

Tomorrow an investigator with a receiver in his car would pick up a designated truck, tail it and photograph the receiver of the pilfered goods. Uncle Barney had arranged for round-the-clock surveillance of Subby and Novak. We would each take a shift.

THE SURVEILLANCE TEAM had nothing to report on Friday morning. Neither man had left his house during the night. Neither had received a visitor. After a hurried conference, Uncle Barney suggested I attend the T.G.I.F. with my Tri State coworkers.

Alfonso's Bar, where the thank-God-it's-Friday crowd met after work, catered to Tri State personnel as well as to the employees of several small factories near the warehouses. The saloon didn't pretend to be anything but a strictly functional drinking place, featuring a long bar, several booths and tables facing it. The bartender, a man with pronounced jowls and sad eyes which lent him the mournful look of a bassethound, had probably heard of a Brandy Alexander and a Singapore Sling, but hadn't been asked to fix either since bartender school. His clients drank beer and shots with an occasional gin and tonic thrown in.

Not to tax his ability and also to keep a clear head, I ordered a gin and tonic minus the gin for me and one with gin for Cathy Carnes. Since I had invited her, I paid for both. I figured I could hold her attention until one of the men had gained enough courage from a bottle to approach her. I offered her my condolences on the death of her mother-in-law.

Cathy thanked me offhandedly, at the same time lifting her shoulders in a shrug. "Her spine got hurt in that accident with Wilma. We had to put her in a nursing home where she drove everybody nuts."

"Maybe she was in pain."

Cathy flashed me a contemptuous look out of bottle-green eyes. "That's what she claimed. But how come the pain disappeared as soon as Tom got there and waited hand and foot on her?"

I had obviously struck a raw nerve. Without waiting

for me to respond, had I even known what to say, she continued, her voice vehement.

"Her complaints stopped the minute Tom got there each day right after work and didn't start again until he got ready to leave her at ten o'clock. He even gave up a good paying job at Tri State to be a short-order cook so that he could have more time to take care of the old biddy."

She paused to light a cigarette. "Do you know what it's like to have your husband spend every free minute with his mother? Do you?" she demanded.

I shook my head.

"Well my husband did that for the past nine months. Nine friggin' long months. It's so unfair. She was a selfish, demanding old witch." Dropping her cigarette to the floor, she crushed it viciously with her shoe. "You think I'm unfeeling and mean, don't you?"

"No." Part of me understood her bitterness. Tom's exclusive, almost compulsive devotion to his mother puzzled me. It was unusual, to say the least, for a grown man to fixate on his mother to that extent.

A truck driver, who seemed hardly old enough to drive much less entertain hopes of winning an experienced woman like Cathy, approached. His clean-cut features and his black cowboy hat made him look a bit like a very young George Strait. The redhead turned her killer smile in his direction which rendered him almost speechless. He stuttered out his offer to buy her another drink. Accepting his offer, Cathy led the bemused man to one of the booths.

Several men bellied up to the bar, including Subby.

"Hey, Elsie," he said, "congratulate me."

"Sure. On what?"

"Our bowling victory. Man, we smoked those guys from Whitman Electric."

"Congratulations." I lifted my glass in a toast. "So, when did this victory take place?"

"On Tuesday evening."

"This past Tuesday?"

"Yup. We bowl every Tuesday, come rain or come shine."

If that was true, it gave him an alibi. "Are all of you on the bowling team?" I asked the men around Subby, trying to verify his whereabouts.

"Yeah. And so's Tully Smith and Lyle Novak. But none of us was as hot as Subby. He bowled a three-hundred game."

"When you're hot, you're hot," Subby crowed.

Tuning out their rehashing of each frame they'd bowled, I considered this new information. Since both my prime suspects had alibis for Tuesday night, a freak accident causing Wilma's death was looking more likely. My gut instincts refused to believe that, but my logical mind couldn't argue with iron-clad alibis.

Several gray-suited men entered the bar. The executives of Tri State joined the workers at the bar. As soon as their notion of propriety allowed, the drivers and loaders withdrew to the tables, leaving Subby and me with the suits. Lyle Novak joined us. If anything was going to change hands, I believed, it would do so in the next hour. I turned slightly away, my body signaling disinterest, but I was short enough that I could catch their partial reflections in the part of the mirror behind the bar not obscured by bottles.

Cathy's young driver dug quarters out of the front pockets of his tight jeans and fed them into the jukebox. The twangy, despairing wails of a female country singer added to the steadily increasing noise level so that I only heard snatches of Subby and Novak's conversation.

"Tonight?" Novak asked.

"Yeah. That damn…"

I couldn't understand the mumbled name.

"…wants it tonight," Subby added.

"…have no choice…."

"…meet at the warehouse at nine."

Expectancy tightened my scalp. I hardly dared to breathe for fear that I might miss something. What was going down at nine? Whatever it was, I planned to be there to see it.

Another wave of happy-hour patrons entered, crowding the bar. Now I was not only unable to overhear Subby and Novak, it was getting increasingly difficult to keep a watch on them. Just as I was getting seriously alarmed, I spotted Uncle Barney. Wearing a conservative business suit, he blended into the crowd of unwinding executives. We both watched for twenty minutes before we saw Novak move toward the far end of the bar to get the bartender's attention. He called loudly for another drink. As he did so, he leaned against the bar, close to a man I had once glimpsed in the main offices of Tri State. Novak's left hand skillfully took a white envelope from his inside jacket pocket and passed it to the man who slipped it into his suit coat. The transfer took perhaps three seconds, suggesting practice. Very smooth.

I looked at Uncle Barney. He inclined his head slightly, signaling that he had also seen the transaction.

Noticing Cathy head for the ladies' room, I followed her. While she repaired her makeup and I brushed my hair, I popped the question.

"Cathy, do you know the guy's name at the bar who works at the main office? He's in his late forties, trim, wearing a gray plaid suit and gold-rimmed glasses?"

"That's Crawford. Galen Crawford. Head accountant. Did he hit on you?"

"No."

"You aren't…um…interested in him, are you? He's married, but that doesn't keep him from flirting and hitting on women whenever he can," she warned.

I saw her giving me an assessing look in the mirror.

"He…um…usually likes 'em younger."

At thirty, I wasn't exactly over the hill, but I didn't say so. "Does he have children?" I asked.

"Yeah. Two boys in college." She turned to look at me directly. "He's not a bad guy, if you're interested. He's rumored to be generous to his women, though a little rough. A friend of mine in real estate just sold him a cottage up at Emerald Lake. Galen's got money."

"I just wondered who he was," I said and shrugged. While Cathy finished applying russet-colored lipstick two shades lighter than her hair, I locked myself into a stall to write a note to Uncle Barney. He needed to know Crawford's name to start the investigation on him. Passing by him on the way back to the bar, I slipped the folded piece of paper into his hand. I thought I was almost as smooth in doing this as the men had been.

I left the bar, a signal for Uncle Barney to follow me. I sat in my car, listening to a symphony on the university's

radio station. I think it was one of Mahler's symphonies.
Uncle Barney joined me a few minutes later.

Bending his tall frame to look through the car window,
he said, "I'll start with Crawford's bank account."

I told him about the conversation I'd overheard.
After a short discussion, I reluctantly agreed that Glenn,
my favorite coworker at the agency, could join me at
nine—even though this sounded a bit like having a baby-
sitter.

My first night of surveillance. I could hardly wait for
night to fall.

THREE

I ORDERED A CARRY-OUT pizza at the Neapolitan. It wasn't just curiosity that took me to the restaurant. Guiseppe made great pizzas. My favorite is the double cheese with fresh basil.

After I ate, I met Glenn in the Kroger parking lot where we left our cars. We jogged past several dark factories, skirted the edge of the airport, and arrived at Tri State five minutes later. Crouching in the shadow of the truck parked nearest the office building, we caught our breaths.

"Damn. I'm going to have to work out more," Glenn panted.

"And quit smoking," I said. Being married to a physician for seven years makes you health conscious.

We sat and waited. Instinctively we shrunk back when the bright headlights heralded the arrival of a car. It stopped. The driver extinguished the lights. Apparently he was waiting for someone. Glenn and I decided that the car was probably a top-of-the-line Buick. It was too dark for us to see the logo. Two other cars arrived, one right after the other.

"Subby and Novak," I whispered, recognizing their vehicles.

The three men converged, then walked toward the main warehouse which Novak unlocked. They came back out a few minutes later, each carrying a large carton.

"Are they taking food home?" Glenn asked.

"That would be stupid. How could they explain having commercial-sized goods if they got caught? You can't buy those at your local grocery."

They loaded the cartons into the Buick.

"We've got to find out who the third man is," I said to Glenn. "I'll follow him and you follow Subby. If we run to our cars now, we should be able to see which way they turn when they pull out of the industrial complex."

Glenn nodded. We ran in a crouch until we reached the edge of Tri State's parking lot. Then we sprinted. Guard dogs barked furiously in one of the factories we passed. I hoped their racket wouldn't summon a squad car.

We made it. Glenn blinked his headlights to show that he had seen Subby's Trans Am turn and was following it. I flashed back that I was on the tail of the Buick which drove north. Keeping a hundred yards back, I doggedly pursued it. The driver kept going north. Consulting my fuel gauge, I hoped he wasn't headed for Michigan. After two miles he turned east on Grover, then south.

The street he took led to only one place: Westport University. I didn't want to believe that someone at the school was buying stolen goods. When he passed the two main dining halls and the student union without stopping, I was both relieved and puzzled. My confusion increased when I tailed him down the main street leading to the residence halls. If I stayed this far back, I would lose him for sure in the maze of buildings once the security guard passed him through the check point.

Making a quick decision, I grabbed my raincoat from the back seat. I flung it over my shoulders, placing its hood over my hair. It wasn't much of a disguise, but the man obviously wasn't expecting to be followed. I pulled up behind him as the security guard raised the guard bar for the Buick. It was too dark to be sure, but I thought the driver was Galen Crawford.

"Hi. I'm visiting Teresa Lister in Beaumont Hall," I told the guard, handing him my driver's license. As far as I knew my friend Teresa was still director of the hall. He placed a visitor's sticker under my windshield wiper and waved me on.

As soon as I was out of the guard's sight, I sped up, praying that a jogger would not decide to dart into the dark road. On the winding road around the lake, I periodically caught a glimpse of the Buick's glowing tail lights. When I reached the straight stretch of the road, I knew I had lost him.

He must have taken one of the side streets. I turned around and drove into the first one. It dead-ended in a cul-de-sac lined by three residence halls: Alpha, Sanccrre and Phillips. Two were men's dormitories, the other a women's. What if the man was involved with a coed, wooing her with jumbo-sized cans of green beans and corn? Unromantic, but possible. If it was Crawford, perhaps his sons lived in one of the male residence halls, and he was taking them food. Why would he? There were no cooking facilities there. Even as I dismissed these ideas as ludicrous, I couldn't come up with a better explanation for his presence on campus.

Slowly I drove along the half-circle. Although I didn't expect to find the Buick parked out front, I wanted to rule out that possibility before I searched the large parking lot in back. Once again his brazenness amazed me. The gunmetal gray car sat in a no parking zone, the trunk open, the motor running. Naturally there was no legitimate parking space in the entire cul-de-sac. I pulled up to a fire hydrant, hoping a campus cop wouldn't choose to patrol the area at that moment.

I rolled down my window. The air was filled with the smell of wet, fallen leaves, of burning charcoal, of youthful laughter, and the sounds of a Rolling Stones song. I hummed along with "(I Can't Get No) Satisfaction." Two young men passed, each carrying a case of Old Style beer. They headed toward the back of Alpha Hall. Moments later three coeds followed, their arms filled with bags of munchies. It didn't take Sherlock Holmes to figure out that a cookout was in progress. I looked at my watch every few minutes. After the third check, the man I awaited came bounding out of Alpha Hall, pulled off heavy, quilted mitts, and slammed the trunk lid shut. The reason he had worn the mitts was to protect his hands from the frozen goods he'd been handling. Probably the steaks which would soon sizzle on the barbecue grills.

When he turned, I saw his face clearly in the light from the nearby street lamp. I had been right. The man who had just delivered the stolen steaks was Galen Crawford.

Subduing my joy at being right, I pondered what to do next. There was no reason to follow Crawford further. Nor could I enter the hall and demand to know who had received three cartons of hot groceries from the head accountant at Tri State. Well, I could, but I had no leverage to force anyone to answer me.

ON SATURDAY MORNING everyone involved in the Tri State case met at the agency. Lynn made a large urn of coffee, set out two dozen assorted doughnuts, a bag of bagels and a tub of cream cheese. Watching her swishing around in her size four slacks, I ignored the pastries, virtuously reaching for a plain bagel. I even passed by the cream cheese without a second glance.

Uncle Barney tacked photos of the receivers of stolen goods on the cork board. Most of the shots were surprisingly good, thanks to the photography course he insists every investigator take. The men stopped milling around the food and sat down. The briefing began.

"We've identified all these men except one: the buyer for the Neapolitan." Barney pointed to the snapshot of a short man with a pencil mustache wearing black slacks and a white shirt, taking a carton of coffee from the Tri State driver. "From the description we have, this could be Guiseppe."

"It isn't," I spoke up. "I've seen Guiseppe at the restaurant. He's older and his mustache is much thicker. Makes him look sort of like a walrus. But this man looks a lot like him. Maybe they're related."

"Okay. We'll attack it from that angle. Jerry, you follow up on the identity of Guiseppe's look-alike," Barney instructed.

One by one the men from the surveillance team reported. Their statements were similar. The recipients of the padded orders signed the official docket and paid for the stolen goods in cash. Half of the drivers handed the cash to Subby, the other half to Novak. Each driver was paid his cut on the spot.

"That way there's no bookkeeping, no record of the illegal transaction. Whoever set this up did a damn good job. And so did you, men. And Cybil. If you've finished your written reports and your expense vouchers, you're free to leave. Thanks."

Lynn spoke up before the men could get out of their seats. "Some of you haven't turned in your listening devices. I must have those before you leave," she said, positioning herself in the doorway as if to block it with her petite body.

Electronic bugs are expensive. One of Lynn's commands is that if you use a bug, you retrieve it no matter how difficult or risky doing so might be. Or you pay for it.

"Cybil, I want to see you in my office," Barney said.

I followed him.

"Glenn reported that his subject stopped off at a bar for a couple of beers and then drove home. How about your man?"

I told him about Crawford's trip to the university. "I thought perhaps he was taking the food to his sons, but they're not listed in last year's directory. Of course, they could have enrolled this fall. The new student list isn't out yet and my contact on campus is out of town for the weekend."

Barney tapped his pipe against his chin thoughtfully. "We've got Crawford as the head honcho in the scheme. Even a quick look at his financial situation indicates that he's spending considerably more money than he earns legitimately. We don't have to solve this little puzzle. He may break down under police questioning and explain it. Still, it's a loose end."

I knew exactly how Barney felt. I hate loose ends, too. "Give me the rest of the weekend to see if I can't resolve this."

"You got it. I plan for us to meet with Ariosto on Monday or Tuesday at the latest to present him with our report."

Back in my office I looked up Crawford's home number. If he answered I'd hang up and try again later. His wife picked up the phone.

"Mrs. Crawford? I'm calling from UMAC Insurance," I ad libbed. "We're offering a special college tuition savings plan for your children. You do have children, don't you?"

"Yes. Two. But they're both in college already."

"Really? May I ask what university they chose?" I wasn't sure she would answer that, but she did.

"My oldest is at Purdue and his brother is at I.U. Both are doing really well."

"That's great. Since you won't need our services, I'll let you go. Thanks for your time." I hung up hurriedly. I suspected she was on the verge of telling me in great detail how well her sons were doing.

So, Crawford hadn't visited his children on campus last night. To whom had he taken the food? I stared out the window for a long time without finding either an answer or a plan of action. The only idea I came up with was to search his office. I would probably find out more at his house, but I wasn't ready to add breaking and entering to my list of investigative accomplishments. Without a doubt, Ariosto would give me permission to search the office. Would that permission stand up in court? I didn't know. Ariosto owned the building, but Crawford occupied the office.

My best bet to get into Crawford's office without arousing suspicion was to masquerade as a cleaning woman. I telephoned Ariosto, told him of my plan without going into details and asked him whether the cleaning crew did the Saturday cleaning that evening or on Sunday. He didn't know, but assured me he would find out fast. He called back within five minutes. The cleaning crew started on Sunday evening at eight.

That worked well with my weekend plans.

WEARING JEANS AND A flannel shirt over a T-shirt, a kerchief tied around my head and yellow latex gloves on my hands, I let myself into the main building. I spotted the cleaning crew, three men and one woman, seating themselves around a table in the lunchroom. A full pot of coffee and a plate of sandwiches told me that they would be there for at least ten minutes.

Crawford's desk was locked. However, the lock was a joke. Even wearing the thick latex gloves, it took me only a minute to open it with my skeleton keys. I searched the contents quickly but methodically. The only interesting thing in the desk was a half-empty bottle of Absolut vodka. Flipping through his appointment calendar, I noticed personal notes. One red, "Get b. gift for Mary." The notation, "Flowers—Ardway," appeared at least every other week. Someone was being showered with

flowers from the most exclusive florist in town. That
could be a lead, I thought.

I checked his closet, emptied the pockets of the raincoat hanging there, flipped through the half dozen books
on finance and accounting on the bookshelf, crawled
under the desk to see if anything had been taped to
the bottom, turned the umbrella stand upside down and
found nothing.

Refusing to believe that there was nothing to be
found, I sat in Crawford's chair, letting my eyes examine
each wall, each piece of furniture. I had checked them
all. I even looked under the blotter, a place so obvious
that no one would hide anything there. When I lifted it,
the photo of his family tipped over. As I picked it up, I
noticed that the fall had dislodged the cardboard backing. My fingers were clumsy because of the protective
gloves. I couldn't get it back into the frame. Curious, I
looked under the backing and eased out what had been
hidden there. The folded piece of paper, roughly three
by five inches, contained dates in the left-hand column
with sums of money in the right column. At the bottom
he had written the four-digit number 5682.

I knew I was taking a risk when I made a photostatic
copy. No sooner had I returned the original to its place
than I heard voices in the reception area. Frantically,
I looked around. There was no place for me to hide
except in the closet. Standing as far back in the corner
as I could with the raincoat pulled in front of me, I
heard footsteps, trash cans being emptied, the vacuum
cleaner springing into action. My heart plummeted to
my toes when the closet door opened and the sweeper
made three half-hearted passes into the closet. Even

after the door closed and the sweeper stopped, I could feel sweat pouring down my back.

Although the crew had finished Crawford's office, it would take them an hour or more to finish the other offices on this floor. I would have to dart in and out of rooms to reach the exit to the parking lot undetected. Halfway down the hall I heard a door open. I crouched beside the water cooler. Fortunately the man in matching gray work pants and shirt turned back to the room to speak to his companion. That gave me enough time to duck into the conference room, praying that this was not next on their agenda to be cleaned.

Standing beside the closed door my heart pounded so loudly I feared the man passing by would hear it. His footsteps continued past the door and out into the parking lot. Great. Now I was trapped until he returned. The room was faintly illuminated by the powerful security light just outside the window. I turned to evaluate my surroundings.

My heart stopped when I saw the figure sitting at the head of the conference table.

Caught.

When I started to breathe again, my heart hammered against my ribs so hard my chest ached. My knees almost buckled, my mouth dried up, my voice failed. I waited a beat, but the figure at the head of the table said nothing. Although I couldn't distinguish his features, the breadth of his shoulders suggested to me it was a man.

I tried to speak again. "Good evening." My voice sounded weak and squeaky. The figure remained silent, unmoving. I have a keen sense of smell which isn't always a blessing. What I smelled made my scalp tighten and the hair at my neck stand up. It was a purely atavistic reaction for I could not identify this odor. I took several steps toward the man. His eyes were open, staring at me.

"I came in here by mistake. I'm sorry." His unblinking stare unnerved me. "Are you all right?" I walked up to him. It was Galen Crawford. "Are you ill?" I reached out and touched his shoulder.

His body fell forward, as if filmed by a slow-motion camera. Or so my brain perceived it. When his face hit the table, I winced. For a moment I didn't recognize the wet-looking stain covering his neck or the gray-white wormlike substance that protruded where his hair should have been. Then I knew. The scream rising in me couldn't squeeze through my tight throat. My stomach heaved in protest. Pressing my hand against my mouth I backed away, unable to tear my eyes from the grisly sight. I kept backing away until I bumped into the door. I tore it open and ran outside.

I kept running until I hit the fence at the edge of the parking lot. Clutching the cool chain links with one hand, I swayed. My stomach violently rejected all I had eaten. I continued to heave long after there was nothing left to expel. When I was finally able to stop, I collapsed with my back against the fence. At first I concentrated on breathing deeply, on regaining some control over my shaking body.

When the trembling ceased, I tried to put my thoughts in order. Galen Crawford was dead. There was no question about that. Nobody could live with only half a head. Remembering, nausea rolled through me, threatening to make me sick again. I shut my eyes, fighting it. Although I eventually managed to subdue the nausea, I knew I would never be able to forget the ghastly image of that bloody body.

The police. I had to report Crawford's death. No, I couldn't do that. They would want to know what I had been doing in the building. On the other hand, I didn't have to tell them my name. Grabbing the fence, I pulled myself to a standing position. My knees almost buckled under me. I clutched the wire mesh and hung onto it. Taking deep breaths, I willed myself to stop shaking. Then I staggered unsteadily to my car and managed to drive to the public phone booth outside the Kroger store. I didn't dare use my cell phone. The cops undoubtedly had Caller ID.

My voice sounded surprisingly steady when I reported the location of the body. When the police dispatcher asked my name, I hung up. Digging through my purse I found another quarter. Uncle Barney's line was busy. Damn. I had to talk to him, to ask his advice. Realizing that discussing a dead body would be better done face-to-face, I got into my car and drove to his house.

Uncle Barney lives in the old, elegant part of the city. Ordinarily I enjoyed looking at the giant oaks shading the Victorian mansions, but not tonight. I willed myself to see the pavement, the traffic signs, not Crawford's bloody head. When I reached his front door, I pounded the lionhead door knocker against the oak until he opened the door. I practically fell into his arms.

"Cybil? What's wrong?" Putting his arm around my waist, he half-carried, half-dragged me to the leather armchair in his living room. "You look awful. What happened?"

"I found Crawford. He's dead. Murdered."

"Good God. Are you sure he's dead?"

I nodded. "The back of his head is missing."

"Jesus." Barney crossed to the liquor cabinet. He poured a half inch of amber liquid into a glass and held it to my lips. I drank the bourbon, feeling a fiery, welcome warmth spread all the way to my toes.

"Now tell me everything from the beginning," Barney said.

I did, ending with the anonymous telephone call to the police. "Did I do all right?"

"Yes. Yes." Glancing at my hands, he said, "You obviously didn't leave any fingerprints."

I hadn't realized I was still wearing the latex cleaning gloves.

"Did anyone see you run out of the building?"

Shutting my eyes, I pictured my headlong flight. "I don't think there was anyone in the hall."

"Good. We'll leave it as is for now. If someone ties you to the scene, we'll say you panicked."

"Which happens to be the truth. All I could think of was to get away from that sight as fast as I could. I'm sorry. I should have telephoned the police from one of the offices."

"It's okay. This was your first encounter with a dead body. Most people would panic."

"I bet you didn't."

"You would lose that bet, Cybil. It happened in 'Nam. I staggered off the road and threw up like a sick puppy."

It was good to hear that my reaction hadn't been unnatural or particularly cowardly. "What do we do now?"

"I'm taking you home. Everything else we'll face tomorrow. I have to make a quick phone call before we leave. Excuse me, Cybil."

I leaned back in the chair. Uncle Barney was back in a minute.

"I expect I'll rate a visit from Sam since we told him about our investigation at Tri State," he said.

I groaned. Sam and I rarely saw eye-to-eye on things and now that I was working for Barney, we disagreed even more often.

"I'll try to keep him away from you as long as possible," Barney promised as he drove me home. I don't remember anything about the drive to my house.

When we got there, Luke was waiting for us.

"I phoned Luke," Barney said, his voice apologetic.

Luke took one look at my face and his eyes grew bleak. I don't know what Barney said to him, but Luke helped me undress and put me under a hot shower. When I had warmed up, he helped me into a flannel night-gown and brought me a mug of hot milk with cinnamon sprinkled on top. I tasted it. "What else is in here?"

"A few drops of brandy."

I looked at him questioningly, knowing he doesn't approve of hard liquor.

"For medicinal purposes," he explained. He watched me drink the doctored milk, waiting.

"Want to tell me about it?" Luke asked after a while.

I shook my head.

"Do you think that's fair, Cybil? You come home in shock, looking like death warmed over, and expect me to go on as if nothing has happened?"

He was right. I told him about finding the body, omitting everything else. To his credit, Luke didn't ask questions or deliver a lecture. He put his arms around me and held me until I fell asleep.

I HAD HOPED THAT THE bright morning sunshine would mitigate the horror of the night before, but it didn't. If anything, violent death seemed even more obscene in the face of daylight. Involuntarily, I shuddered.

"I made breakfast," Luke announced, setting the tray on the nightstand.

"Thanks. You stayed the night?"

"On the sofa."

He filled a cup with coffee and gave it to me. It was strong, the way we both like it. Luke set a toasted whole-grain English muffin before me. "Luke, I can't eat."

"Yes, you can. It's easy. Watch me."

His strong white teeth took a bit bite out of his muffin. Then he pushed the pot of honey toward me, his eyes challenging me to refuse to eat. I broke off a tiny piece and put it into my mouth. Eventually it disintegrated and I swallowed it.

"I can't eat," I repeated. "Just because you're used to seeing torn-up human beings doesn't mean the rest of us are."

"Whose fault is it that you found that body?" Luke countered. "Your own. If you'd taken a suitable job you would have spared yourself this ordeal."

"Look, I'm not complaining or whining about my

job. All I'm saying is that I don't feel like eating, and missing one meal isn't going to have any long-range negative effect on my health."

"Suit yourself. I have to get to work." He walked toward the door.

"Luke, thanks for staying. I appreciate it," I called after him.

He stopped and turned. He looked at me with unreadable eyes. Then he nodded and left.

I'd hurt his feelings. I felt like the ingrate he probably thought I was. I'd have to find a way to make it up to him.

FOUR

I SHOWERED, MADE A HALF-HEARTED attempt at curling the ends of my hair with the curling iron, dressed in moss green corduroy slacks, a matching silk blouse and low-heeled suede boots. From the hall closet I grabbed a jacket.

Since I'd left the rental car at Uncle Barney's house, I drove the Volvo. I had forgotten what a comfortable ride it provides.

Lynn was measuring coffee into the filter when I entered the office. She paused to survey me.

"You're early. The coffee should be ready in a minute. How are you feeling this morning?"

From the way she asked, I knew Uncle Barney had told her about last night. "I'll make it."

"I'm sure you will. Most of us do."

And that's all the sympathy I'd get from her. Frankly, I was surprised she had even asked how I was. I watched the dark liquid begin to trickle into the pot.

"I still remember my first air raid," Lynn said, her voice low.

I wondered if the planes had belonged to North Vietnam or to the U.S. To the dead that had undoubtedly not mattered. Lynn seemed lost in thought, so I kept quiet. The only sound in the room was the dripping of the coffee. When it stopped, I held out my mug, the one

Maxi had given me with the chubby Kliban cats on it for her to fill. I took it to my office.

Since I'd taken on this assignment a week ago, two people had died violently. One accidentally. Maybe. The other... I raised my hand to the back of my head, holding an imaginary gun.

"What are you doing?"

Uncle Barney stood in the open door. I hadn't heard him approach. "Trying to see if Crawford could have shot himself."

"And?"

I shrugged. "I'm no expert on gun shots, but blowing off the back of one's head is an awkward way to commit suicide."

"It would be more natural to hold the gun to the temple or fire it into the mouth," he said.

"If I'd kept my wits about me, I would have looked around for a gun."

"What else did you notice last night?"

I thought about the still figure sitting in the chair and it hit me. "He didn't shoot himself. If he had, he would have fallen forward, or sideways, wouldn't he? Somebody arranged him in that chair, and that rules out suicide," I said, pleased with my reasoning.

"I'd say so. It'll be interesting to find out if he was shot in that room or somewhere else."

"But why bring him back if he was killed at another location?"

"Because the murder scene might point to the identity of the murderer. Or maybe he or she thought the body wouldn't be found until sometime today. It's unlikely that the conference room would have been cleaned unless it was used, and it's doubtful that a meeting was held on Saturday. From what we know of the Tri State operation, only a skeleton crew works on weekends and that's mostly in the warehouses. Crawford, as the chief accountant, wouldn't have been expected in the office. Perhaps the murderer needed time to establish an alibi. He or she couldn't know that you would stumble on the body."

I sat, thinking about what Barney had said.

"By the way, what makes you think Crawford was shot?"

"I guess I assumed he was," I admitted. "What else could have been used to take off part of his head? It didn't look bashed in. "I felt a little queasy thinking about that head.

"Never mind. The police will establish what killed him. Come and help me work on the report."

From the way he changed the subject, he must have noticed my reaction. "Wait. There are two more things you ought to know." I told him about Crawford's flower orders and about the hidden slip of paper. I took it out of my shoulder bag and handed it to him.

"It looks to me like blackmail payments he received or paid."

"Received, I think. One of the women at work said that he recently bought a cottage on the lake, and that he has a reputation for being generous to his women. At least to the ones he cheated on his wife with. What do you think that four-digit number means?"

Barney squinted at the number thoughtfully. "It could be a locker number. Maybe a safety deposit box. It's too short for a zip code, a phone number, a lottery ticket or the combination to a safe. I'll have Lynn make a photocopy and place the original into the vault. It could be something simple and obvious that escapes both of us right now."

"Before we start the report, I want to call the florist and try something." Glancing at my watch, I said, "They open in five minutes."

Barney nodded and left. That's the great thing about him. He doesn't insist on knowing the methods his investigators use, so if one of us does something that backfires or misses, we don't have to confess our failure. He trusts us to stay inside the law, but how we get results is up to us.

Promptly at eight I dialed the florist's number. Pretending to be young and flustered, I said, "Hi. I wonder if you can help me. I'm sort of in a tough spot. I'm filling in for a friend and her boss, Galen Crawford, told me to order the usual flowers from you on Friday, but I forgot. And I forgot to ask him who gets the flowers. If I ask him this morning, he'll know I messed up and he'll be so mad at me. Can you help me out?"

"Let me check the rolodex. Yes. Galen Crawford. A dozen red roses to Jennifer Wooster. I can send them first thing this morning. No problem."

"Oh thank you. You saved my life."

Asking for Jennifer's address might have aroused the woman's suspicions. I reached for the phone book. There were only three Woosters listed. Fortunately, Jennifer was one of them. Since I'd done so well with the florist, I decided to try something with Jennifer. I dialed her number.

"Good morning. This is the Central Consumers'

Club. We're going a survey and if you could answer three questions it would help us tremendously. Also we'll send you a free gift. First, are you between the ages of twenty and thirty-five?"

"Yes."

"Are you married or single?"

"Single."

"Where do you work?"

"Tri State Personnel Department."

Surprise, surprise. An office romance and red roses. Galen Crawford had not been an imaginative man.

"Thank you so much. Have a nice day," I crooned, hanging up before she could question me about anything.

When I went looking for Uncle Barney, Lynn informed me that he was in conference and that I was to start on the report alone. Writing reports isn't my favorite thing to do but it's part of the job. By noon I had finished the rough draft. I placed it on his desk before I went to lunch.

Since I was alone, I bought two Cambodian egg rolls and Jasmine-flavored tea from the little booth in the square. I carried my lunch to the bench in the courtyard, enjoying the perfect late autumn day. Most likely there wouldn't be many more.

I brooded about the Tri State case. I wasn't happy with it. Barney had decided to close it. And he was right. We had accomplished what we had been hired to do: expose the theft ring. But two people had died violent deaths during our investigation. That's what bothered me.

Even though I knew the police would mount an

inquiry into Crawford's death, they were satisfied with the ruling of accidental death in Wilma's case. I was not. She wasn't careless with her wheelchair. And she wasn't suicidal. I had been a counselor long enough to spot the signs of suicidal depression.

Before driving to Ariosto's house, I brushed my hair and freshened my makeup. A protective act, I reflected. If I ran into Pauline I didn't want her perfectly groomed, pampered appearance to make me feel inadequate.

Expecting Brazier's thin, bent body to open the mansion's door for me, I was caught off guard when I came face-to-face with the best looking young man I'd ever see outside the movies. I suspect I stared at him round-eyed until he spoke.

"You must be Mrs. Quindt. My stepdad is holed up with his lawyer for another ten minutes. Will you come in and wait? I'll keep you company."

He flashed me a smile of singular sweetness that made me swallow twice. I was married and ten years older, but still the young man caused me to catch my breath. I felt a rush of compassion for all those twenty-year-olds out there who had few if any defenses against his beauty.

"I'm Harry Ariosto."

"Cybil Quindt." We shook hands. I followed him into a game room down the hall.

"I remember you," Harry said. "You were one of my sister's friends. Well, Annette isn't my blood sister, but I always think of her as my big sis."

I was flattered he remembered me. Vaguely I recalled a boy of seven or eight, hovering in the background, shy and perhaps a little lonely in this huge house peopled by adults. He certainly wasn't shy anymore.

"Can I get you a drink?" Harry asked.

"A soft drink, if you have it."

Harry busied himself at the elaborate wet bar flanking the south wall.

"Aren't you going to offer me a drink, too?"

Startled, I turned in the direction of the voice. A big armchair swiveled around to face us. In it Pauline Ariosto lounged, her legs crossed, her thighs scantily covered by her short denim skirt. With the third button of her white silk shirt undone she looked, I thought, like a woman trying to be deliberately provocative.

"Don't you already have a drink?" Harry asked.

"Not anymore." Pauline raised an empty glass and wagged it at him. The movement caused several bracelets to clink against each other.

"It's still early. Don't you think you ought to go easy on that stuff?"

His voice sounded pleading, I thought.

"Don't you tell me what to do, too. Just fix me the damn drink."

Harry's face flushed, his eyes narrowed. For a second they glowered at each other, the tension between them almost palpable. Then Harry took a decanter, splashed some of its colorless liquid into a glass, added tonic water and a slice of lemon. He brought me my cola before he handed the vodka tonic to his stepmother who thanked him with exaggerated politeness. I felt acutely uncomfortable as if I had walked into an ongoing quarrel.

Harry took a can of beer, popped the tab, and drank deeply, almost defiantly.

No one said anything. I wanted to be almost anywhere but in that tension-filled room.

Ariosto came in, looked pointedly at his wife's drink, his mouth thinning with disapproval. "Isn't this a little early, even for you?" He turned to Harry. "Don't you have classes today?"

"Yes. I came by so Sidney can look at my car."

"Sidney's my chauffeur, not your mechanic. Take your car to a service station."

I could sense Harry's embarrassment clear across the room.

"Cybil, are you ready?" Ariosto asked.

"Yes." All I wanted was to get out of that house.

Without another word, Ariosto started toward the door. I murmured goodbye to Harry and to Pauline and followed him. The man would never win a prize for manners or warmth.

In his study I handed him the report. While he read it, I watched his face turn livid, his hands tighten on the sheets of paper. I was glad we no longer lived in an age when the messenger of bad news was summarily executed.

Whipping his glasses off, he tossed them on the desk. "There's one thing I regret—that Crawford isn't alive so I can have the pleasure of firing him and pressing charges. That rat. One of my top men, and he screws me."

An interesting reaction, I thought. Ariosto considered the pilfering a personal affront. No regret over Crawford's death, only that Ariosto could not administer the punishment himself.

"You did a good job, Cybil. I won't forget that."

No, he wasn't a man to forget anything. The moment he handed me the check covering our fee and expenses, I left that tension-filled mansion as fast as I could without actually breaking into a run.

AT THE AGENCY Lynn pounced on me the moment I walked through the door.

"About time you got here," she hissed, her black eyes snapping. "Barney's had to face them alone."

"Face whom?"

"The police."

Uncle Barney stood up when I entered the conference room where he was meeting the police. He doesn't do this in the ordinary course of a business day. I suspected he wanted to convey a message to Sam and his companion about how to treat me. Both men stood. Sam introduced me to Sergeant Griffin, a thin-faced man whose red, raw nose indicted he was suffering from a head cold. Being susceptible to colds, I sat as far away from him as I could.

"Did you submit the report to our client?" Barney asked.

"Yes. The account is settled."

Barney nodded, satisfied.

Sam broke into the conversation. "As I said before, this is a murder investigation. The usual client confidentiality mumbo-jumbo doesn't apply."

Sam looked ill-tempered, harried. Maybe the investigation into Crawford's death wasn't going well. Or maybe he was catching his partner's cold.

"I realize that," Barney said, his voice quiet. "But it would be helpful if you gave us some information in return. You know, the old 'you scratch my back and I'll scratch yours'."

"All right," Sam agreed, not too graciously.

Barney reported our findings. The only time he consulted the pages in front of him was to get the name of the drivers and the receivers of the stolen goods.

Sergeant Griffin was taking notes furiously.

"That could be a motive," Sam said, "thieves falling out among themselves."

"From our superficial check on his finances, it seems to me he took in more money than could have been his share from the pilfering," Barney said.

"What are you suggesting? Blackmail?"

"In a setup like that, it wouldn't be impossible. By the way, what killed Crawford?"

"A shotgun blast. He must have been in the act of turning his head. He was hit from the side."

"Was he killed where you found him?" Barney asked casually.

Fortunately Sam wasn't very perceptive and so he didn't catch that keen interest masked by a nonchalant tone. I kept quiet. When you have something to hide, be inconspicuous.

"No. He was killed somewhere else," Sam said.

"Time of death?"

"Sometime early Sunday evening. You certainly are interested in details," Sam said, his eyes narrowed in suspicion.

"Professional curiosity." Barney kept his face blank.

"A woman reported finding the body. Would you know anything about that, Cybil?"

"Me? Find a murdered body?" I asked, injecting disbelief in my voice. I met his eyes squarely. Then I shivered visibly, hoping to put him off without actually having to lie.

"You worked at Tri State. What's the gossip about Crawford?"

I decided to tell the truth about this. Crawford's womanizing could be a motive. Some cuckolded husband or lover could have decided to put an end to his tomcatting. "Well, he's supposedly cheated on his wife and according to rumor, he is…was generous to his lovers."

Between sneezes the sergeant made a note of that.

"Were any of the women at Tri State involved with him?"

"You'll have to ask them that yourself," I said.

Sam sent me one of his hard looks which did absolutely nothing to intimidate me. I suppose someone brought to the police station might feel a stab of fear, but it's hard to be intimidated by someone you remember wetting his pants at age five while running away from a spooky house on Halloween night.

"Where were you Sunday night?"

I had braced myself for that question from the moment I entered the conference room. "Let's see," I said, pretending to think back. "I cooked supper, cleaned up after I ate, drove to the store, read and went to bed around eleven." Except for omitting a couple of things, all of that was true.

"Any witnesses?"

"At home? No. At the store? I don't know if the cashier will remember me or not."

"What do you suspect Cybil of?" Barney asked. "Surely you don't think she shot Crawford?"

"No. But I wouldn't put it past her to find the body, phone in a report, and then disappear."

"Are you charging Cybil with anything?" Barney demanded, a hint of steel in his voice.

Sam backed off. "No. I have no proof. The cleaning crew saw and heard nothing."

That was welcome news. I was careful to keep my face blank. I looked at the carpet. It really was a lovely Oriental rug.

As soon as they left the conference room, I slumped in relief.

"Do you think Sam will check my alibi?"

Barney shook his head. "No. He didn't even ask the name of the store."

"Phew. I'm glad that's over."

"You did very well."

"Thanks. So, where do we go from here?"

"A new case."

"But we can't," I protested and then shut my mouth. Officially we were finished with Tri State.

"What's bothering you?" Barney asked.

I shrugged, feeling foolish. "I guess I want to get everything solved, including Crawford's murder, but I know that's now up to the police."

Barney fiddled with his pipe, clearly waiting for me to get something off my chest.

"Oh, all right. Crawford's unexplained trip to the university still bugs me and so does Wilma's death."

"That's been ruled accidental, so unless you come up with concrete, new evidence, we'll leave that alone. As to Crawford's visit to Alpha House, you can pursue that but in down time."

"Thank you."

FIVE

IT HAD BEEN SEVERAL days since I'd seen my grandmother.

I dialed Maxi's number on my cell phone. She was at home, baking apple strudel.

"If you have time, why don't you come by for a piece? As late as you eat supper, you won't spoil your appetite."

"I'll have to finish some paperwork, but then I'll be there." For Oma's strudel I'd walk the five miles to the farm. Barefooted, if necessary.

I finished the reports and took them to Uncle Barney's office. When I told him that I was on my way to Maxi's farm, he told me to give his mother a hug from him.

Maxi lives on a small farm south of town. Until I got married and had a home of my own, her house was the place I loved most in all the world. Memories of my father who was killed when I was four, are dim at best. The only places I remember are the apartment my mother rented before she remarried and the three houses each subsequent husband provided for her. They were houses, not homes. I know the difference well.

Even though Maxi bakes delicious pastries and bread from scratch, she's not the typical old-fashioned storybook grandmother. For one thing, she holds strong opinions on everything, informed opinions, because she reads all the time. She always has. Years before feminism came into its own, Maxi refused to allow men to congregate at one end of her living room and women at the other. She had six children whom she loved fiercely, but she refused to allow them to become her one topic of conversation or the sole focal point of her life.

"Being a mother ought to make you more knowledgeable of the world around you, not less," Maxi has said many times. "How else can you guard your babies and raise them to become intelligent, worthwhile human beings?"

I had planned to raise my child like that but I wasn't given the chance. Quickly I flipped on the radio. The sweet strains of a Haydn piece washed over me, not lessening my pain, but distracting me a little from it. I concentrated on the music, listening for the woodwinds. I focused so hard I almost missed the turnoff to Maxi's farm.

The house looks like old farm houses did before brick ranches replaced them: narrow, tall in front with a couple of one-story additions in the back. The wooden frame was painted white, the roof covered with green shingles.

Automatically I walked around to the back. The only time I can remember entering through the front door was when I brought Luke to the farm for the first time.

Maxi was waiting for me.

"The coffee is ready and so is the strudel," she called to me from the kitchen sink where she dried her hands on a dishtowel.

"Mmm…nothing beats the aroma of freshly brewed coffee, apples and cinnamon."

"Sit, sit." Maxi had cleared the table after her frugal evening meal and covered it with one of her lovely embroidered cloths. She poured the dark liquid into the fragile porcelain cups with the gold border. Delicate violets ringed the outside. I remember impatiently waiting for the day when I would be old enough to drink out of this cup.

"Uncle Barney sends his love," I said, accepting a piece of strudel.

"So, why didn't my son come?"

"He was still busy at the office."

"Ha! With that *Drachenliebchen*, no doubt."

There's no good translation for that word. Perhaps dragon lady comes closest. Maxi, who is a truly accepting, tolerant person, does not like Lynn. I think Lynn feels the same way about Maxi. Maybe it's because both women are fiercely protective of Uncle Barney. Maybe it's because neither wants to share him with the other. Maybe it's because they're both strong women who are a lot alike. Sometimes I suspect that the dislike is rooted in something that happened in the past.

"How is work?" Maxi asked.

"Fine."

"But?"

I can hide little from my grandmother. Her intelligent blue-gray eyes miss nothing. I told her about the Tri State case and my reservations about it. I could see she was thinking furiously about something.

"What is it?"

"Wilma Johnson. That name is so familiar."

I told Maxi about the accident.

"Of course. Mae Carnes. That's the connection. I'll get my scrapbook."

Ever since she retired as reference librarian from the Westport Public Library, Maxi has been keeping scrapbooks of newspaper clippings on people she knows. Having lived in Westport for over forty years, she knows a lot of people.

"Here it is," she said, carrying over a big album. She removed the clipping and handed it to me.

"Did you know Mae died last week, Cybil?"

"Yes. Her daughter-in-law told me."

"That still surprises me. That Tommy got married. That he broke away long enough from his mother to find himself a wife."

"How well did you know Mae?"

"Not well, and that was a long time ago. Her husband and mine worked together at Studebaker. Before that they'd been friends in high school. The men wanted us to be friends, too, so we could go out together, but Mae couldn't bring herself to leave Tommy with a baby-sitter. He was too frail and too high strung, she claimed." Maxi shook her head.

"If you ask me, the only thing wrong with the boy was that Mae spoiled him rotten and smothered him. I used to see them at company picnics over the years. Tommy was a real mama's boy, hardly left her side." Maxi refilled my cup. "So, what are you going to do about Wilma?"

"I don't know. I have no evidence, just a hunch."

"Don't fret, *Schatzi*. If there's something fishy about

her death, someone will make a mistake, and you'll spot it."

"Thanks for the vote of confidence." Maxi has always supported me in whatever I've wanted to do. Sometimes I think she believes there's nothing I can't do. I saw her glance at the kitchen clock. It was almost time for the PBS evening news. Maxi never misses it. She doesn't even answer the phone or the doorbell while the program is on.

"I'd better get home. I have to do some laundry," I said.

"I wrapped up some strudel for Luke and for Barney." Maxi handed me two foil-wrapped packages from the counter.

Was this a ploy so that I had to go and see Luke? I looked at Maxi carefully. No. She simply liked him, and knowing how much he loved her baking, she wanted to share it with him.

"Thanks, Oma. This will make both of them happy." I kissed her cheek.

I STOPPED AT THE CAMPUS cafe and bought two take-out lattes. Then I drove to the hospital, taking a chance on Luke's still being there. He was. I'd forgotten how good he looked in the lime green scrubs.

"Are you all right?" he asked, his voice concerned.

"I'm fine."

"No aftereffects from the shock of finding that body?"

"None that I'm aware of. I visited Maxi. She sent you some strudel. And I brought a couple of lattes. Do you have time to take a break?"

"For strudel? Are you kidding?" He turned to the nearest nurse. "Marlene, I'm taking a break in my office. So unless there's a catastrophic emergency, don't call me."

The nurse promised, giving me a sly look.

Luke led the way. He moved a bunch of medical journals from the visitor's chair and motioned me to sit.

I set out the coffee and handed him the foil-wrapped plate. He sniffed and sighed happily. I watched him eat the strudel with so much enjoyment it made me smile.

"When was the last time you ate?" I asked him.

"Strudel? Not since the Labor Day picnic at Maxi's farm. Cafeteria food? At noon, I think. It was so unmemorable that I'm not sure."

"Hospital food hasn't improved any, huh?"

"No."

Our eyes met. We both remembered the years of his residency and the countless times I'd come to the hospital to eat the tasteless food so that we could spend some time together. I felt the burning ache in my throat that always preceded tears. Quickly, I suppressed the memory of our early years.

"Would you like this last piece?" Luke asked.

"No, thanks. I ate so much strudel at Maxi's that I'm not only going to skip dinner, but I'm also going to the YWCA to swim laps. I can't afford any more calories."

"You look just fine to me."

The way he looked at me, made me feel warm all over. Time to leave.

"I'd better go. Maxi gave me some strudel to deliver to Uncle Barney."

"Cybil, thanks for bringing me this treat. I'll call Maxi to thank her."

"She'll like that. She always enjoys talking with you."

I SPENT TUESDAY IN FRONT of the computer, doing research for other cases the agency handled.

On Wednesday Maxi phoned, saying she had to come to town and could I meet her for lunch at her favorite place, the restaurant in the Nightingale Hotel? Of course, I agreed.

We chose a booth in the corner. When we were seated, Maxi looked around.

"When I first came to Westport, the Nightingale was the best hotel in town. It was during the last years of the depression, so not too many people could afford to stay here. I remember once the Laubensteins invited me to lunch on my birthday. I thought there couldn't be a fancier place than this hotel in all the world."

I watched Maxi's face soften with her memories.

"It's a shame the city let the hotel degenerate into a… well, during the sixties it was little more than a trysting place for illicit lovers. It's now trying to make a comeback."

We ordered hot tea with our chef salads. Maxi considers most restaurant coffee undrinkable.

"What a coincidence," Maxi said, craning her head. "There is Tommy Carnes. We were just talking about him the other day."

I turned my head in the direction of Maxi's gaze.

"Behind the counter," she prompted.

"Cathy, his wife, told me he worked as a short order cook so he could spend more time with his mother."

"That figures. She was the type to use whatever she could to get her way," Maxi said.

Wearing a chef's hat and apron, Tom looked younger than I had pictured him. He would have been a good-looking man except for his petulant expression and his big ears.

"Excuse me, dear. I'll just go and say hello."

I watched Maxi talking to Tom. She returned within minutes.

"He remembered you from the Studebaker picnics?" I asked.

"From his mother's funeral. I would have recognized him anywhere though."

"How is he?"

Maxi looked thoughtful. "That's hard to say. He always was a bit of an odd duck. He's…distracted. Like only part of him is here. There's also a gray aura about him. I don't like that gray aura."

I waited for Maxi to elaborate. She didn't. From what I remembered about auras, a gray one wasn't good. Poor Cathy. I hadn't liked her at first, but after I found out about her home life, I understood her better. All her flaunting was a desperate attempt to reassure herself as a woman.

We enjoyed our lunch. Maxi talked about her early years in this country. I never tire of listening to her.

LUKE'S PARENTS HAD GIVEN us season tickets each year to the football games at the university. Since o separation, we split the tickets. I had invited Joan, whom I've known since high school. She's a loan officer in Westport's biggest bank and an avid football fan. The home team pulled an upset, giving everyone hope for an invitation to the Fiesta Bowl. Afterwards we dined at the Brauhof Restaurant, drinking imported Stiegl beer and eating excellent pot roast.

THE RED LIGHT ON THE answering machine blinked furiously when I arrived home. The two messages were from Terrance Ariosto, asking me to come to his house as soon as possible. The first had been left at five-thirty, the second an hour later. I thought his voice sounded urgent, perhaps even worried, but with an authoritative voice such as his, it's hard to tell.

I exchanged my suit for jeans, a white turtleneck with a jewel-toned challis scarf, and a suede jacket. Looking in the mirror I thought I looked all right except for my hair. It was beginning to rain which always makes my hair go out of control. Something about the humidity. I gathered it up, twisted it into a knot at the back of my head and fastened it with half a dozen hairpins. I grabbed my shoulder bag and my raincoat and drove to Ariosto's.

On the way I tried to guess what he wanted with me, but had no clue. Crawford's murder was a police matter and the pilfering case had been solved. At least to Uncle Barney's satisfaction, if not to mine. All that was left unexplained was Wilma's death which kept bothering me . . . . . . to reach mosquito bite.

. . . . the circular drive and walked up

to the door. I rang the bell. No one came. I knocked harder. To my surprise, the door opened a few inches.

"Hello," I called out. No answer. I called again, louder this time. I was sure I could be heard in the far reaches of the house. Hesitantly I pushed the door open. The elegant entry before me was dimly lit by two tapers on the wall but empty. The house was silent. That was odd.

The house was unlocked with the lights on; and somebody ought to have been home. Certainly Ariosto, who had phoned me twice, asking me to come. Where was Brazier? Besides him, the household staff included the cook, Mrs. Dougherty, as well as the chauffeur whose name escaped me just then.

I proceeded toward Ariosto's study down the hall. Here the door was ajar, too, light spilling out into the hall.

"Mr. Ariosto?" After waiting a few seconds, I pushed the door open wide enough to step inside. I sensed movement to my left but before I could turn, I felt as if the roof had collapsed on my head, burying me in darkness.

I DON'T KNOW HOW MUCH time passed before I became aware of pounding pain in my head.

From far off I heard groans. It took a while before I realized they were mine. Raising my head, I saw the polished hardwood floor pitch and heave. Nausea surged through me, forcing me to close my eyes and lower my head back down to the floor.

I fought the nausea, the dizziness, the pain. My fingers burrowed under the twisted knot of hair to find a throbbing lump that seemed to grow even as I explored it with gentle fingers.

Great. I probably had a concussion. Luke was going to love this.

The smooth floor felt cool beneath my cheek. As long as I didn't move, I could endure the pain. Tempting as it was, I couldn't remain there. Who had hit me? Ariosto? No, that made no sense. He had summoned me. Who then? Was that person still in the house? For the first time since I'd regained consciousness, alarm surged through me. I had to get up. Find Ariosto. Phone the police and report the assault on me.

Slowly, inch by inch, I pulled my upper body into a sitting position, fighting nausea all the way.

When I opened my eyes, I wished I hadn't. A few feet away from me sprawled the body of a man. Even though he lay face down, I knew it was Ariosto.

I half scooted, half crawled toward his outflung arm, searching for a pulse. Finding none in his wrist, I touched his throat. Nothing. That's when I saw the puddle of blood under his upper body. At the same time I became aware of that sweet, sickly smell I had noticed in the conference room where I had found Crawford.

My heart started to pound painfully, echoing the pounding in my head. Still, I wouldn't, couldn't, panic this time. Carefully I lifted up Ariosto's shoulder and looked at his chest. That was a mistake. The room spun crazily. I let my head drop back onto the floor. I wasn't going to pass out, I vowed.

I looked at my watch. Surprised, I discovered that I'd been unconscious for mere minutes. I was fairly certain that the person who hit me was gone. Why should he, or she, stick around? Still, I listened intently for several seconds. The only noise I heard was the humming of the far-off furnace.

The telephone. I pulled myself up, using the desk. Leaning halfway across the desktop, I dialed the emergency number, requesting an ambulance and the police. While I was still holding the phone, I dialed Uncle Barney's number, praying he would be home. He picked up the receiver on the third ring.

"Uncle Barney, I'm sorry to bother you at home, but I need your help," I said, speaking slowly and carefully. I heard a low voice in the background. Female. Not pleased by the interruption. Lynn?

"Is this really important?"

"You tell me, Uncle Barney. I'm in Ariosto's study. He's lying in his blood on the floor. I have a lump the size of a ping pong ball on my head, and I've called an ambulance and the police, but I don't know if I'm going to pass out before they get here."

"Is Ariosto dead?"

"Yes. His chest…." I gagged and pressed the back of my hand over my mouth. "There's so much blood," I said, my voice weak.

"Hang on. I'll be right there."

SIX

KNOWING THAT UNCLE Barney was on his way, I imme-diately felt better. Not much, but some. I had to concen-trate on something other than the body on the floor.

Looking around the study I saw a cart by the window loaded with glasses, decanters and an ice bucket. I zeroed in on the bucket. Removing the scarf from around my neck, I wrapped ice cubes in it and placed it on the bump on my head. The throbbing in the lump lessened.

All the glasses on the cart were placed upside down on a snowy linen napkin. All except one. It was empty. Ariosto's glass? I doubted that because on his desk sat a squat tumbler containing a small amount of amber liquid in it.

The deep windowsill behind the cart was covered with travel brochures. Most of them advertised ocean cruises. Was Ariosto planning to take Pauline on a cruise? Where was Pauline anyway? Where was the rest of the household?

I took a pencil out of my bag and used it to move the brochures around. I could explain my fingerprints on the telephone and the desk, but not on the brochures. I found a slip of paper with a telephone number on it and some notations that looked like dates and times of departure. I copied them into my little notebook. There was also a program of the Chicago Symphony, my very favorite.

I noticed that it featured Daniel Barenboim conducting Beethoven.

The last time I'd found a body I panicked and ran. This time I would use my chance to look around until the police arrived. Was anything out of place? Missing? I had been in this study several times. The room obviously hadn't been ransacked.

Using my pencil I pulled out the middle drawer of the desk. It contained nothing out of the ordinary. The left drawer held a metal cash box. I expected it to be locked but it wasn't. After a quick count I estimated that it contained about eleven hundred dollars in cash. The motive for the murder had not been robbery. The right drawer was locked. That piqued my interest. Why lock it and leave the cash box open?

I studied the lock. For a wealthy man, Ariosto certainly hadn't paid to have good locks installed on his desk. It took only three keys on my skeleton ring to open the drawer. Somewhat surprised, I stared at the hanging file folders. What was so important in them that they had to be locked up?

Ariosto was…had been an orderly man. Each file was labeled with a tab. Reading them, I discovered that they referred to members of his family and household. I scanned the contents of the folders until I heard the distant sound of a siren. Quickly I closed the drawer, locked it, and scooted around the body without looking at it.

The first person who entered the house was Lieutenant Sam Keller, my cousin.

Two medical attendants carrying a stretcher rushed in behind him. I directed them to the study.

"Cybil. What are you doing here?" Sam demanded. "The dispatcher said somebody's been hurt or killed. Who?"

"Terrance Ariosto."

Sam whistled. "Boy, you don't fool around with small fry, do you?"

I opened my mouth to reply, but thought better of it.

"Follow me," Sam ordered.

I did. Sergeant Griffin, blowing his nose, trailed close behind me. In case I decided to bolt? Both men entered the study, but I waited in the hall. The sight of Ariosto's body was indelibly imprinted on my brain. I didn't need to see it again.

I walked to the bottom of the elegant, curved staircase and collapsed on the second step. That's where Uncle Barney found me a few minutes later.

"You okay?" he asked.

I nodded. "The body's back there." I pointed down the hall, "and so's Sam."

"I'll be right back."

Uncle Barney returned shortly and sat down beside me. "Let me look at you." Gently he touched the back of my head, feeling for the bump. He couldn't miss it. "Maybe we ought to have this looked at before anything else."

"No. Later. Maybe."

"Do you see double? Have trouble focusing?"

"No. If I have a concussion, it's a mild one. Remember, I'm married to a doctor. I've learned a few things in our years together."

"I just wanted to be sure. Ariosto's not a pretty sight. Sure you're okay?"

"As okay as anyone can be under the circumstances. Do you think he was killed with a shotgun like Crawford?"

"Seems that way to me. The autopsy will say for sure."

"Both deaths have to be connected, but how?"

"I have no idea. Yet. Tell me exactly what happened."

"Yes, I want to know that, too," Sam said, walking up to us. "Let's go into the parlor or whatever this room is called." He led the way into the living room. "Sit down," he said, pointing to a sofa.

I sat.

"Well, I'm waiting," he prompted.

Sergeant Griffin flipped his notebook open, ready to record whatever I had to say. I told them exactly what had happened, starting with the telephone message on my machine.

"What did Ariosto want with you?" Sam demanded.

"I don't know. We finished our investigation for him days ago. Unless it had something to do with Wilma's death. Or Crawford's."

"I told you there was no evidence of foul play in her death," he snapped. "And we're investigating Crawford's murder. Anybody else hear this so-called telephone message?"

"It isn't so-called, and it's probably still on the answering machine tape. Why don't you go and check it out?"

"I might just do that." Sam paced the length of the room. "Let's go over this again."

"Let's not. My head hurts."

"You might have left something out."

I groaned, pressing my hands against my temples.

"Okay, okay. Let's skip to when you got here. Are you sure there was no one else here?"

"I was at the time. Now we know that the person who hit me over the head was still in the study. He or she was probably the same person who killed Ariosto."

"Anything to indicate whether it was a man or a woman?"

"No."

"Did you hear a shotgun blast?"

"Is that what killed him?" I couldn't repress a shiver.

"Probably. Did you hear it?"

"No. When I arrived, everything was quiet, but all that means is that the murderer had already shot Ariosto."

"Let's try to pin down the time you arrived. When did you get here?"

"I didn't look at my watch when I left home, so I can only guess. I must have left between seven thirty-five and seven-forty. It takes fifteen minutes or so to get here. That would make it seven-fifty or fifty-five."

"Then what? Wait. Why don't you show us what you did and we'll time you."

Reluctantly I went back outside and reenacted my arrival.

"Okay." Sam looked at his watch. "That took only two minutes. The dispatcher recorded your call at five after eight." Sam paced some more. "Cybil, think back carefully. You said you checked Ariosto's pulse. Was he still warm?"

I must have looked sick, because Uncle Barney protested the brutal question.

"Look, we're trying to establish time of death. Usually we have to rely on the autopsy report which gives us a range of hours at best. This time, though, we lucked out. The way I figure, Cybil must have arrived moments after the shotgun blast. Think, Cybil."

"I don't know. He…he wasn't cold or stiff."

"What color was the blood?"

I pressed my hand over my mouth, fearing I might get sick.

"Look here, Sam. Cybil's in shock and in pain. Ease up."

"I can't. This is too important."

I waved my hand for them to stop. "I'll answer. I remember that Ariosto's white shirt was bright red in front. Not rusty brown."

"Good work, Cybil. That means the blood hadn't started to coagulate. That puts the time of death as no earlier than seven-forty and no later than seven-fifty-five. Good, good."

Sam seemed inordinately pleased. I was fairly certain that no physician would narrow down the time of death that closely based on the evidence he had, but I said nothing.

"Cybil, what did you see when you pushed the door to the study open?" Sam asked.

"Nothing. The world caved in on me."

"Are you sure? Think back."

"I saw the door. The dark wood. I pushed it farther back…then nothing."

"He or she must have stood pressed against the wall, arm raised." Sam demonstrated. "As soon as you pushed the door open, wham!"

I flinched when his arm came down forcefully. "What do you think the assailant hit me with?"

"The skin wasn't broken on your scalp," Barney mentioned, "but that's because your thick coil of hair protected you. Could have been almost anything. The butt of a shotgun even."

"The murder weapon?" I asked.

"Could be," Sam agreed. "Did you hear anything when you came to?"

"No."

"You didn't hear a car start?"

"No. But I was out cold. He could have driven off during that time."

"Was there a car parked out front when you arrived?"

"No. But it could have been parked in back where the family's cars are kept. Or even farther back by the stables. You wouldn't hear a whole fleet of cars start from there."

"Where does that back road lead to?" Barney asked.

"Out to Locust Road. I remember leaving once that way after I'd gone horseback riding with Annette."

"Locust connects with major roads going east and west," Sam added. "The murderer could have gone any-where from there. Sergeant, make a note to check that area first thing in the morning. Get it roped off now."

Sergeant Griffin left immediately.

"Okay. You didn't see or hear anything. What did you touch in the study?"

"The edge of the desk. I needed it to help pull myself up. And the telephone."

"Anything else?"

"No. I used my scarf to remove the lid to the ice bucket." I told Sam about the improvised ice pack which since had turned into nothing more than a sopping wet scarf.

"You called the operator and Barney. Why did you call him?" Sam demanded.

"Because I was scared, alone, and in pain. I needed a friendly face."

"Why not call your husband?"

A fair question, I thought, but Luke was the last person I would call under such circumstances. He hated my job and would never forget this incident. Aloud I said, "You know Luke and I are separated. I don't call him when I have a problem."

"Why did Ariosto call you?"

"I already told you. I don't know why. He just left a message to come here."

"Isn't it unusual for him to call you to his house?"

I shrugged. "Not really. I reported to him at his house when we investigated Tri State. He liked meeting here. When you have as much money as he does, you can summon people anywhere you want."

Sam grunted.

Just then two men wheeled a stretcher through the hall. On it lay Ariosto's wrapped figure. The last time he'd leave his house, I thought. Tears rose in my eyes.

For no reason that I could fathom, I started to cry. Seeking to comfort me, Uncle Barney put his arm around my shoulders.

"I have to take Cybil home. Luke will have my hide if she doesn't get medical attention right now."

That seemed to work. Sam gave permission for Uncle Barney to escort me home. He helped me into his car.

"I'm taking you to the emergency room," Barney said.

"No! Under no circumstances. Uncle Barney, I don't have the kind of concussion that needs hospitalization."

"Then I'll call Luke to come to your house to have a look at you. I don't want to hear any argument about that."

Whenever Uncle Barney used that tone of voice, it was useless to argue.

I must have dozed off, for the next thing I knew, he had pulled into my driveway. He led me onto the porch where he took the key from my purse and unlocked the door.

"Wait," I said, knowing I had left a ladder in the foyer. I switched on the light and headed straight for the sofa in the living room.

"You've made some progress," Barney said, looking at the walls from which I had stripped four layers of wallpaper. He used his cell phone to call my husband.

Luke arrived only a few minutes later. He must have been at the hospital which is only six blocks from my house.

To my shame, I used my injury to act more groggy than I really felt. It saved me a lot of questions I didn't want to field. Luke was great. He examined my lump, shone a light into my eyes, checked my reflexes and announced that I had only a minor concussion, which I already knew. I perked up some. Suddenly I wanted to talk.

"Who do you think killed Ariosto and why?" I asked Uncle Barney.

"That's hard to say. Any man who acquires that much wealth also acquires enemies."

"Business enemies?"

"Probably. Personal, too."

"Ex-wives," I murmured.

"There are times when a husband is justifiably tempted to do in not only an ex-wife, but a current wife as well," Luke muttered meaningfully. He unpinned the knot of hair that had saved me and placed an ice pack on my head. He raised my hand and put it on the bag to hold it in place.

His hands were gentle, I noticed, though his voice was not. I grabbed his hand and pressed it. "Thank you."

"You're welcome."

"Not too many people will benefit financially by Ariosto's death," I said. "Certainly not Pauline."

"How do you know that?" Luke asked.

Uncle Barney leaned forward, waiting to hear my answer as well.

"I saw the prenuptial agreement she signed."

"Where did you see that?" Barney asked.

"In his desk. Don't worry. I didn't leave any prints."

"Jesus," Luke said, staring at me as if I'd suddenly sprung horns.

"Good girl. What else did you see in the desk?" Barney asked, directing a brief, apologetic look at Luke.

"That's it, Barney. It's bad enough that you encourage Cybil in this investigating business, but now you've gone too far. She should have been resting an hour ago, not answering asinine questions and doing God knows what." Luke stood up, glowering at Barney.

"You're right. I'm sorry," Barney murmured, his voice meek. "I got carried away. I'll talk to you tomorrow, Cybil. Now you've got to rest."

I didn't want to rest. I wanted to talk. I was all wound up. Luke put an end to that speedily. Next thing I knew he'd shoved a pill into my mouth, forced water down my throat and had me lying in bed, wearing nothing but my underwear. The last thing I remember was him tucking the down comforter around me.

Time passed in a haze of headaches, interrupted sleep, and brief moments of wakefulness. During these moments I remember Luke checking my eyes, asking me how I felt and Maxi putting damp, cold cloths on my forehead with murmured, calming words.

When I finally woke up with a clear head, I could tell by the light in the room that it was late. I turned. My head still hurt and my mouth felt cottony but the nausea was gone. The glittery hands of the crystal clock on my nightstand told me it was eleven-fifteen; the date indicated that it was Monday.

Luke had kept me in bed around the clock, justifying his decision by his belief that rest is a great healer. Maybe so, but I had a lot to do. Just to be on the safe side, I called his name twice. When he didn't answer, I crawled out of bed. If I hurried I could be up, dressed and looking perfectly well by the time Maxi came to check on me.

I took a shower, turning the water to lukewarm because hot didn't feel good on my bump even though it wasn't as large as it had been the night before. Even so, I shampooed gently around it. By the time I had dried myself and put on a robe, I didn't feel that great anymore. I curled up on the love seat in my bedroom. The air will dry my hair, I thought, closing my eyes and drifting off.

The moment Maxi walked into the room I woke up.

"Stay put," she said. She sat down beside me, checked the back of my head and my eyes. Then she stroked my hair.

"How do you feel?" she asked.

"So-so," I answered truthfully.

"Luke said to keep checking your eyes. He also said to remember that the human skull is pretty sturdy, but not indestructible."

I nodded slightly.

"Can you eat something?"

The idea didn't appeal to me particularly.

"At least a bowl of soup," she cajoled. "I'll go and fix it."

It was about noon. I had hoped to make it to the office by one. Maybe if I ate something, I might feel stronger. Holding onto the walls, I inched my way into the kitchen.

"Cybil, I was going to bring the food into the bedroom," Maxi said, her tone chiding.

"You know I don't like to eat in bed. Food always gets on the sheets." Looking at the crackers she'd placed on a plate, I added, "I hate crumbs in my bed. They feel like pebbles."

I sat down at the kitchen table which faces the backyard. The brilliant red of a cardinal caught my eye. I looked for his mate. I spied her sitting on a branch of the lilac bush.

"Here it is. Chicken soup. Doesn't it smell good?"

"Yes, it does." I managed to eat most of it, pleasing Maxi tremendously. Afterwards I lay down on the sofa, planning to get up as soon as Maxi finished cleaning up. I didn't. When I awoke again it was four. I felt better. I telephoned the office, asking Lynn to let me speak to Uncle Barney.

"So, you got yourself in trouble again," she said in lieu of a greeting. "Barney has been on the phone with the cops most of the day. And we had to send someone to fetch your car from the Ariosto place and drive it to your house."

Her tone implied unmistakably that all that was my fault. Before I could stop myself, I murmured an apology, but at least she put me through to Uncle Barney without further comments.

After answering his inquiries about the state of my health, I asked, "What's new on the Ariosto case?"

"Officially the cause of death is a gunshot wound, as we suspected."

"Where was everybody last night?"

"Pauline and Harry were in Chicago. They returned late. The staff had the night off."

"All at the same time?"

"Yes, and it struck me as being strange, too," Barney admitted.

"Maybe Ariosto wanted everybody out of the house when he talked to me. But why would he?"

"I don't know unless it was something of a sensitive nature."

"Such as?"

Barney was silent for a beat. "It would have to be personal, I think."

"About his family?"

"Yes. Maybe about Pauline."

Now I was getting where he was heading and I didn't like it. "You don't suppose he wanted me to follow her?" To spy on lovers was a truly repugnant idea. Even if the lovers were carrying on an illicit relationship. My instant, relieved reaction was that I wouldn't have to do it now.

"It could have been about an employee in his house," Barney added.

"True." Brazier? Unthinkable. Mrs. Dougherty? Unlikely. The chauffeur? I hardly knew him. That automatically moved him to the top of the list. Pauline and the chauffeur? No. The idea was ridiculous. What's-his-name was hardly a handsome youth, as I remembered him. Pauline wouldn't risk her marriage and its bejeweled compensations lightly. She had struck me as a shrewd, levelheaded woman not given to rash impulses.

"You mentioned a prenuptial agreement last night. What else did you see?"

"As I said, Pauline doesn't profit by Ariosto's death.

Harry's got a hefty trust fund, so he gains nothing either."

"Not unless Ariosto disinherited him."

"He couldn't. Harry's adopted. In our state you can't disinherit adopted children," I reminded Barney.

"True. Who else was mentioned?"

"Ariosto's nephew, Ramsey, who gets a chunk of cash but also receives a block of stock for each year he works for Ariosto. I doubt that he would cut off that desirable perk."

"And his daughter?"

"Annette inherits big, but I can't see her shooting her own father. Besides, she married money." I thought for a moment. "You think the two murders are connected?"

"Crawford's and Ariosto's? They could be."

Uncle Barney was silent. I imagined him toying with his unlit pipe, the way he does when he's concentrating.

"I keep thinking about Crawford's blackmail. If only we knew what that four-digit number was. That has to mean something," I said.

"I agree. We'll keep working on it. In the meantime, you stay home and get well."

I remained seated by the telephone, thinking. After a while I removed the notebook from my bag and stared at the mysterious numbers: 5682. I added the digits. I subtracted them. I averaged them. I pretended they stood for letters of the alphabet which gave me EFHB. That didn't mean anything either. At least not to me.

Feeling physically better but thoroughly frustrated, I pulled on jeans and a sweater and drove to the nearest place with public lockers: the airport. Identifying myself to the head of security, I asked him about the locker numbers. My digits were out of his range. The same thing happened at the bus station and at the post office. I phoned my friend Joan. Even though she was a loan officer and didn't deal with safety deposit boxes, I thought she would know. She told me that the safety deposit boxes at her bank consisted of four digits and one letter of the alphabet.

Passing one of Westport's high schools, I made an illegal U-turn and went to consult with the assistant principal. Their lockers consisted of three digits only as did the lockers of the other four high schools in the city. I had ruled out all public places in less than two hours. With my strength flagging, I drove home for another nap on the sofa.

Maxi brought supper from the farm, claiming that there was nothing in my larder fit to cook. From a gourmet's point of view, she was probably right.

SEVEN

At the agency Glenn and the other operatives were solicitous, Lynn distant. I tried to explain to her that if Ariosto had called Uncle Barney he would have gone to his house, too. Somewhat frustrated by her lack of response, I added that it wasn't my fault our client got himself killed. On a logical level Lynn had to agree with me, but she wasn't ready to let me off the hook yet.

At the staff meeting Barney wrote the puzzling number on the board, soliciting everyone's input.

"A numbered account in a Swiss bank," Glenn guessed.

"Too short," Barney said.

"Maybe the number of a receipt," I offered. "You know, like from a pawn shop. Maybe a place that repairs things."

"Could be," Barney agreed. "Glenn check it out."

That damned number had to be important. Why else hide it behind a picture?

Barney asked me to go to lunch with him which earned me a reproving look from Lynn. Since it was a working meal and I wasn't wasting my uncle's time with personal matters, I smiled blithely at her as we left.

We went to The Upstairs, an excellent restaurant catering to the business crowd. The place was jammed with dark-suited men. The occasional woman present was also conservatively attired, but not me. I was wearing a paisley-print challis dress in shades of blue and purple with a dirndl skirt and ruffles around the high neckline, topped with a short boiled-wool jacket the same color as the brightest violet in the dress. I felt like a cheerful peacock among a flock of somber crows.

After we ordered, a turkey club sandwich for Barney and a spinach salad for me, we concentrated on our problem.

"We've got two men killed with the same weapon, presumably by the same person. The connection between the victims is Tri State. One of them is involved in theft and blackmail," Barney summarized.

"The question is, whom is he blackmailing and why?" I added. "At first I thought Crawford might be blackmailing Ariosto who got fed up with the blackmail. They had a confrontation, and Crawford killed him, but his own murder rules that out."

"I agree. There's a third person involved with both of them."

"Our only clue to that person so far is that mysterious number and the money paid to Crawford. Then there's Wilma's accident," I answered.

Ignoring the reference to Wilma, Barney said, "Sam found out that Crawford opened a savings account in his name only in July. All the deposits to this secret account were made in cash."

"Blackmail money."

The waitress served our food. A few minutes later she brought me a folded piece of paper bearing a telephone message. "Annette Ariosto has called twice. She wants to see me urgently," I read aloud.

"Finish your salad first," Barney ordered. "She can wait a few minutes."

"I wonder what she wants," I murmured. Thoughtfully I speared a hot bacon dressing-covered piece of spinach. "I'm sure it's not a social call." We ate in silence, each of us wondering about Annette's call. Neither of us lingered over lunch or asked for dessert.

Back at my desk I dialed the number Annette had left. Like her father she came straight to the point when she answered.

"My attorney advised me to hire you, Cybil. Are you free to accept the assignment?"

"Well, yes, I think so, but why does he want you to hire me? Annette, your father was murdered. This is a police matter."

"They suspect me and Ramsey," she blurted out.

"You're… I was going to say kidding, but naturally you aren't. Are you sure about their suspicions?"

She laughed bitterly. "I only wish I weren't."

"Why do they suspect you?"

"Can you come to Dad's house? I don't want to talk about this over the phone. There are too many extensions in this house. Someone might eavesdrop."

In her suspicions, too, she was like her father. "Sure. When do you want me to come?"

"Right now."

"I'll be there in less than thirty minutes." Briskly I brushed my hair, applied lip gloss and ran to Uncle Barney's office, bypassing Lynn's desk. I heard her hissed exclamation but ignored it because I knew he was dying to know why Annette had called.

"Her attorney advised her to hire us. She's a suspect, she claims, and so is Ramsey."

"Interesting. What does she want you to do?"

"She wouldn't tell me over the phone. I'm on my way to the house now."

"Our legal system provides for the defense of all suspects, even the guilty ones."

I waited for Uncle Barney to continue. When he didn't, I said, "I'll tell her that if I find evidence pointing to her guilt and if the D.A. or the cops ask me about it, I'll have to reveal it."

"Yes. She needs to understand that."

"If after I talk to her I think she's guilty, I'll turn down the case. Is that acceptable to you?"

"Eminently."

"Good. I'll report to you after I get back." I was glad Uncle Barney isn't one of those unethical private investigators who give the profession a sleazy reputation.

ONCE AGAIN I PARKED THE Volvo in front of the mansion. Brazier let me in. He even remembered my name. As he escorted me to the morning room, I asked, "Brazier, what's your regular day off?"

"Sunday. You are wondering where I was Saturday night?"

"Well, yes. When I arrived none of the staff were here to let me in."

"Mr. Ariosto insisted we all take the evening off."

"Did he insist on that often?"

"No, ma'am. I recollect that happening maybe two or three times in the twenty years I worked for him."

"Did he say why he wanted you all to have the night off?"

"Mr. Ariosto wasn't in the habit of explaining his orders, Miss."

Of course, not. How dumb of me to think he might have had the courtesy to do so.

Annette stood by the bay window gazing out over the covered swimming pool. She was smoking one of her long, thin cigarettes. We greeted each other, but she didn't offer to shake hands. I didn't think she had changed a lot, but then her tall, angular, well-groomed, expensive look ages well. Compared to the hard glamor of Pauline who lounged in a love seat, Annette appeared understatedly elegant.

"You mind going for a walk?" Annette's question was a mere formality. Already she was reaching for a mink-lined car coat.

"No," I said, not having a choice. Not that I minded the walk.

Outside she set off quickly toward the stables, her shoulders hunched against the wind, her hands buried in her coat pockets. I pulled the hood of my coat over my head, waiting for her to speak.

"I can't believe any of this is happening," Annette burst out at last. "It's like a nightmare. First Dad gets himself killed. Then the cops are continuously around, snooping, prying, insinuating."

At the stables, Annette pulled the huge door open. Even though there hadn't been horses around for several years, the stables still smelled faintly horsy.

"I wish Dad hadn't sold the horses. Some of my happiest times were spent here."

Annette walked past the empty stalls, obviously re-membering their former occupants. I followed her, still waiting for her to tell me what she wanted me to do.

"But I guess without anybody riding them, there was no sense in keeping horses."

"Harry didn't like to ride?"

"No. As a boy he was afraid of them. Dad tried to cure him of his fear by putting him on Red Thunder, but Harry ended up bawling like a baby."

That must have been the equivalent of tossing someone who is afraid of water into the deep end of the pool. Head first. I remembered Red Thunder as a nasty-tempered, overfed, baleful-eyed beast whom I avoided at all cost. Whenever I saw Ariosto at the stables which, thank heaven, hadn't been often, he slyly offered to saddle up Red Thunder for me. His idea of a joke, I guess.

Stopping at the last stall, Annette lit another cigarette, sucking at it greedily. I stepped back to avoid being enveloped by smoke.

"You asked me why the cops suspect me. One reason is that I inherit most of Dad's property."

She said that defiantly as if expecting me to cluck disapprovingly or make some guilt-inducing comment. When I didn't, she continued.

"My God, as if I were poor!"

"There's more to it, isn't there, though?"

"How clever of you," she flung at me.

Her tone was mocking. Now I remembered that she'd been sarcastic and sharp-tongued in high school. I ig-nored her sarcasm. After all, she was paying for my services, she was still in shock from her father's murder, and she was scared. I remained silent, waiting for her to continue.

"All right, if you must know," she added, her voice and expression testy, "Dad and I had a row the last time I was here."

"A row?"

"Okay, a fight. A shouting match. But we always shouted at each other when we argued. Naturally the hired help overheard and told the cops. Couldn't wait to tell them I'm sure."

"What was the fight about?"

"Do you have to know that?"

"Since it seems to be the reason the police suspect you, yes."

"It was about money. See, as soon as I mention money you get that aha-she-did-it look in your face, too."

"You must admit it's an unfortunate coincidence."

"Tell me about it." She took another deep drag on her cigarette before she ground it out with her high-heeled boot. "Anyway, it wasn't as if I needed or wanted the money for myself. I had an opportunity to invest in a really promising venture and I didn't have enough cash of my own."

"And your father refused to lend you the money."

"Yeah. He claimed the investment was too risky. That's just because he was so conservative and he didn't know Sasha who is a great designer. His clothes are really fabulous. All he needs is a little capital to get his first collection out and he'll be off and running. It was practically a sure thing."

Personally I didn't think that anything in fashion was a sure thing. From what I'd heard, haute couture was almost as risky a venture as opening a new restaurant. "How much did you ask for?"

"Only five hundred thousand. It wasn't as if Dad couldn't afford that. But no, he didn't trust my judgment."

Because she was involved with this Sasha? Judging by her passionate tone and expression the designer must mean a lot to her.

"Anyway, Sasha managed to get by on the two hundred and fifty thousand I had, so it didn't matter in the end. I certainly couldn't kill Dad for a measly half a million."

I believed her. Anyone who could refer to half a million dollars as measly, didn't need the money desperately. Besides, I always thought she loved her father. "Is that all the police have on you?"

"Well, no."

I hadn't thought so. "What else is there?"

"I don't have an alibi for that evening."

"Since you live in Detroit, it would take longer than an evening to get to Westport and back."

"I was alone that evening and that night."

I kept looking at her, waiting for an explanation.

"The kids were staying with my husband's parents, and he was on a business trip. I gave my housekeeper the night off. I felt like being alone."

She was lying about that. Her body language betrayed her.

"You don't believe me, do you?"

"I believe you did not kill your father."

"But?"

"You're not telling the complete truth about your alibi."

"Thanks for believing me about Dad."

"Annette, I can't help you if you don't level with me."

"I'll tell you this much. I...I wasn't alone."

The implication was obvious. She'd been with a man. Sasha?

"I won't admit that to the cops. I just can't. You've got to help me."

"I'll try. You said the police suspect Ramsey, too. Do you know why?"

"Uh-huh. He had an argument with Dad at the office. Dad threatened to fire him, but he did that regularly, every two months or so for the past ten years. Ramsey didn't shoot Dad. Except for me, my cousin was one of the few people who really liked my father. Dad argued with everybody. That in itself didn't mean a thing."

"How did he get along with Harry?"

Annette shook her head. "Harry never learned that you had to stand up to Dad. If you didn't, he rode rough-shod over you. Grit was the only thing he respected."

"And Pauline?"

With a dismissing gesture, Annette snorted. "I gave that marriage another six months at most. She didn't care about Dad. Only about what she could get out of being Mrs. Terrance Ariosto. Just like his third wife."

Annette's mother, the second Mrs. Ariosto, had been killed by a fall from a horse. I don't remember her. In high school when I used to come to the house, the third Mrs. Ariosto had been in residence. She had reminded me of a small, compact dynamo, always in motion.

"What was your stepmother's name?" I asked.

"Which one? Mrs. Committee?" Again Annette's laughter was bitter. "Lucinda. That woman had time for everything and everyone except the people in this house. Convenient for her to forget that charity starts at home. Harry could have used a mother a whole lot more than Westport needed a super committee woman."

"Where is she now?"

"I thought you knew. She died six years ago, so you can scratch her off your list of prime suspects. Besides, I can't imagine her capable of enough passion or anger or hate to kill anyone."

"Whom can you imagine as the murderer?"

"That's just it! I've thought and thought about that. There isn't anyone except…."

"Except?" I encouraged.

"Dunn, the chauffeur. I guess Dad finally had enough of his unreliability and fired him. He told Dunn he wouldn't work in this town again. He was lucky Dad didn't call the cops on him."

"Why should he have?"

"Dunn was a thief. Dad suspected him for quite a while but he could never catch him. He'd order two cases of Beefeater Gin but received only one. Guess who had the other case?"

"Who would know Dunn's last address in town?"

"Brazier keeps the staff records. Are you going to check on Dunn?"

"Yes. I'll start with him." Mostly because I didn't know where else to begin.

She walked back to the house with me and left me in

the servants' sitting room off the kitchen. Brazier donned wire-rimmed spectacles to look through a file.

"Here we are. Sidney Dunn. 503 South Fourth Street."

"What kind of car does he drive?"

"A Pontiac sedan. Navy blue."

"License plate?"

Brazier looked through the form. "Hmm. Sidney didn't fill that part in."

One of the bells mounted on a board on the wall rang. Brazier glanced at it. "Excuse me," he said, "Mrs. Ariosto needs something."

Though Brazier's face was schooled not to betray any emotion, his voice suggested ever so subtly that Pauline rang that bell quite often.

"Thank you, Brazier. I'll wait for Mrs. Dougherty."

He nodded and left. Moments later she walked in.

"There you are," Mrs. Dougherty said with a smile. She carried a tray. "I saw you walking with Miss Annette. You looked cold. I made us some tea like in the old days."

"Thank you." I gladly accepted the cup she handed me. The tea looked rich like polished mahogany, just the way I like it. "Mmm. Good enough to drink without anything in it," I said, declining her offer of sugar and lemon.

"I'll just take a bit of sugar."

The cooks's bit consisted of two heaping teaspoons. She settled her ample body into the armchair, prepared for a leisurely chat. I had always enjoyed our tea visits while waiting to tutor Annette who was never punctual.

"Miss Annette hire you?" she asked, stirring her tea.

"She did. Do you think Sidney Dunn is a thief?"

Mrs. Dougherty winced at the word. "That's a mighty hard label to pin on a man. I think maybe he wasn't as careful about what supplies belonged to the house, but in an establishment like ours, few employees are that scrupulous about whether they paid for the bar of soap they're using or not. Employers know and expect that. I don't know why the boss suddenly turned on Sidney. He wasn't any worse than anybody else."

"How long have you worked here?"

"I was hired by Annette's mother when she came here as a bride. Now there was a fine woman." Mrs. Dougherty sipped her tea, sunk in memories. Then she roused herself. "You want some cookies? They're store bought, I have to confess, but it doesn't pay to bake in a house where everybody watches calories. Except Harry, and he was never partial to sweets."

"Harry lives on campus, doesn't he?"

"Yes, but he's back here a lot."

Watching her closely, I tried to interpret the undertone in her voice. She really liked Harry. The shy little boy had probably spent his happiest hours in Mrs. Dougherty's kitchen. She would have been happy to have him come home. Yet I sensed…reservations? Disapproval? I couldn't pinpoint the emotion.

"How's Harry doing in school? He's a senior now, right? I saw him the other day for the first time since he's grown up. He's certainly a fine-looking young man," I said.

"Isn't he, though?" she remarked, pleased. Then she sighed. "He's a senior, and he was doing real good till the spring semester. Then his grades took a dive." Mrs. Dougherty shook her pink-beige, fluffy curls sorrowfully.

"What happened?" I asked.

"Near as I can tell, Harry fell in love."

"That happens a lot in college. But grades don't usually drop through the floor."

"When you fall for the wrong woman, everything goes wrong."

Brazier returned, effectively stopping whatever else she might have said.

"Mrs. Ariosto wants a small steak and a salad for dinner, and Miss Annette wants a poached egg and steamed broccoli," he told Mrs. Dougherty.

"A real challenge to my cooking skills," she muttered.

Knowing that I couldn't learn anything else, I thanked her for the tea and left.

Brazier saw me to the door. "Miss Annette has hired me to look into what's happened. Tell me about Dunn's leaving," I requested. Brazier obviously didn't want to answer my question, but knowing that Annette had hired me, he did.

"Well, there was a case of gin still in the trunk of the limousine when Dunn went off duty."

"He could have left it there by mistake."

"Maybe." Brazier shrugged.

"So Dunn might have been fired even though he could have been innocent?"

"Innocent isn't a word I would associate with Sidney."

From Brazier's expression I knew he wouldn't say anything else except goodbye.

EIGHT

My NEXT STOP WAS Dunn's apartment. His was the upstairs part of a small frame house that needed a coat of
paint. The entrance to the upper half had been added to
the side of the building, consisting of unprotected stairs
leading to a small landing. I climbed the worn wooden
steps and rang the doorbell. When no one answered, I
pounded on the door. He apparently wasn't home.

Maybe the people downstairs knew something about
his whereabouts. Mounted on a post of the sagging front
porch was a wooden box with Dunn's name stenciled
on it: a mailbox without a lid, overflowing with mail.
Glancing around to see if anyone was watching, I flipped
through the contents of the box, rationalizing that looking at the outside of envelopes wasn't tampering with
the U.S. Postal Service.

Most of it was junk mail, with a few bills. A phone
bill. Master Card. An envelope marked Airport Inn that
looked like it contained a bill. Why would he get a statement from a sleazy motel on the outskirts of town? I
tossed the mail back into the box and knocked on the
front door.

An enormously obese woman opened the inner door,
leaving the torn screen door latched. Even the short
waddle to the front door had left her wheezing. "What
do you want?" she asked, her tone less than cordial.

"Are you Sidney Dunn's landlady?"

She looked me over as if she wondered if I had a machine gun tucked under my coat. Finally she nodded.

"I'm looking for him."

"He ain't here."

"I discovered that already."

"What do you want with Sidney?"

"When will he be back?"

"Don't know. He didn't say."

"Do you know where he is?"

"Nope."

Her voice indicated that she wouldn't tell me if she knew. "How long has he been gone?"

She shrugged. "Three, four days." She looked at me through slitted eyes, partly the result of layers of fat, partly due to suspicion. "You that ex-wife of his who's been dogging him?"

Suddenly the landlady looked even heavier, like an outraged mother hen with her feathers ruffled.

"No. No. The Ariostos want me to talk to him. He used to work for them."

Her tiny eyes glared at me balefully. "Those bloodsuckers? A man works long hours for them with never a word of appreciation and at the first sign of trouble they give him the boot. The rich ain't fit to spit on."

Her version of Dunn's firing was different yet, but like Mrs. Dougherty, she seemed to like the chauffeur.

"I only want to ask Sidney a couple of questions," I said. "Here's my card. If he comes home, please have him call me."

Suspiciously she opened the screen door just wide enough to stick out her pudgy hand for my card.

She didn't say anything but closed the inner door decisively.

Now what, I wondered, standing on the sidewalk. When in doubt, pursue the routine set up for finding missing people. I pulled into the nearest fast food restaurant which happened to be a Burger King and bought a medium diet cola. The place was quiet in the interim between lunch and dinner.

I sat by the window, making notes on the Dunn investigation. It wasn't that I suspected Sidney Dunn of the murder of his boss. I still thought that someone connected with both Crawford and Ariosto had to be guilty of that. But as Ariosto's driver he could possess some vital piece of information.

The Airport Inn. What was Sidney's connection with this questionable establishment? Since I had no other leads, and since I was in the western part of the city, I decided to pay the inn a visit.

Up close the Airport Inn looked even more seedy than it had driving by at forty-five miles per hour. I parked in front of the office. One of the *f*s had been smashed in the neon sign that identified the motel's headquarters. Quickly I scanned the area, hoping no one I knew saw me enter this hot-sheet establishment.

There have been times when I've found the smell of popcorn enticing beyond resistance. This wasn't one of them. Possibly because the butter used in the machine in the corner had been rancid. Possibly because the popcorn maker hadn't been cleaned in recent history. I tried not to breathe. The office was empty, giving me a chance to look around.

Cluttered beyond belief, I almost stumbled over a low

magazine rack. When I noticed the type of literature it held, I gave it a wide berth. The T-shirts hanging on a rack bore slogans I hadn't known were legal to print. Hearing heavy footsteps approach, I faced the counter. That was a mistake. The array of "love aids" as they were advertised in the display case was astonishing: everything from erotic oil to reputed aphrodisiacs to crotchless underwear to black leather items I was too embarrassed to look at closely.

The man's jaded eyes assessed me briefly but thoroughly. Just to set the record straight, I showed him my business card.

"Security Agency, huh? Well, cookie, we don't need no security. There's two of us on duty at all times. We're security enough."

He flexed his arms, threatening to split the Budweiser University T-shirt's sleeves, to emphasize his claim. He probably pumped iron every other day, but that didn't mean he could fight. Still, he looked formidable enough physically that few would challenge him.

"We've got to have our own security, what with our rentals and all."

The rentals he referred to were shelved behind the desk. From what I could see they were all so-called adult videos.

"I'm looking for someone," I said.

"Ain't we all." He grinned briefly, humorlessly, displaying big, yellow teeth.

"His name's Sidney Dunn."

"Never heard of him."

"That's strange. You sent him a bill. Judging by your

establishment, I don't think you give credit unless you know someone."

"Still ain't heard of him."

"Maybe the other security person has."

"Nope. Him neither."

Not only was he lying, he wasn't even pretending not to. That made me angry. "He's wanted for questioning in connection with a murder case. If you'd rather talk to the cops, I can arrange that. Of course, they'll be interested in how many of your guests aren't old enough to buy cigarettes or your magazines or rent your adult videos. Not to mention how many of them have liquor and grass in their rooms." That got his attention.

"Hold on. Let's not be hasty. I know Sid."

"That's better. Where is he? Look, I only want to talk to him. I don't care who he's with."

"Room 21."

"Thank you." For a tough guy he caved in quickly, but I also had a hunch that he would phone Room 21 as soon as I was out of sight. I left my car parked where it was and sprinted around the corner to my destination. I knocked on the door. I thought I heard a flurry of motion behind it before a male voice answered.

"Who is it?"

I identified myself, telling him I wanted to talk to him about Ariosto.

Cautiously he opened the door. The first thing I noticed was that Sidney was alone. The door to the bathroom was closed though. The second thing I noticed was that the room had a definite lived in look: beer bottles and pop cans overflowed from the inadequate trash can, a greasy pizza carton leaned against the wall and the small table was littered with filled ashtrays and crumpled fast food sandwich bags. The room could stand a thorough airing.

I watched Sidney turn down the volume on the television set, silencing a rerun of a game show. Sidney wore brown slacks, a tailored yellow shirt open over a snow-white T-shirt and white tube socks.

Straightening, he faced me, hands on hips. His small, bright, clever eyes watched me with a predator's gleam. The eyes and the ginger hair gave him a slightly fox-like appearance, I thought.

"You heard that Terrance Ariosto was murdered?"

"Yeah. It was on TV. Couldn't have happened to a more deserving guy." Realizing how that sounded, he added, "Hey, that don't mean I killed him. I didn't like him, but I don't know anybody who did. He was a mean, spiteful s.o.b., if you'll pardon my French."

"He fired you, didn't he?"

"Yeah. After fourteen years of toting his skinny butt all over creation he fired me without a recommendation. It ain't easy at my age to get another job without references."

Could that have set him off to come back and blow a hole into Ariosto's chest? I doubted it, but still it was possible.

"Look, lady, I didn't kill him. Sure, I hated his guts. Who wouldn't?"

"Why did he fire you?"

"What did they tell you up at the house?"

"They said Ariosto caught you with a case of gin that belonged to him. Expensive gin."

"Oh, sure. I don't even like the stuff. I'm…"

Why did he look as though he realized he'd said something he shouldn't have, I wondered. "Did you take the gin?"

He lifted his shoulder in a gesture that could mean anything. That, coupled with his closed, obstinate expression, told me he wasn't going to elaborate.

"Where were you on the night of the murder?"

"I don't have to tell you."

"That's true, but you can tell Lieutenant Keller. I'm sure he's looking for you as is your ex-wife." At the mention of the ex, his ruddy complexion paled, it seemed to me.

"That's hitting below the belt."

"Where were you the night Ariosto was killed?"

Sidney sighed. "Right here."

"Can anybody corroborate that?"

"No."

The bathroom door opened a foot. "Sid, we'd better tell her before she sets your ex loose on us."

The female speaker remained behind the door.

"Would you please come out, Miss...?"

"Ms. Clark. Donna Clark," she said, pushing the door open all the way.

A woman in her forties, I judged, whose body was just beginning to thicken around the middle, but who was still attractive. Donna came and stood next to Sidney.

"Sid didn't kill nobody. He was right here with me. I'll swear to that on a stack of Bibles ten feet high."

I wondered what it was about Sidney that made women like him. Then he smiled at Donna, and I knew.

"How can you be sure he didn't sneak out?" I asked.

"The television said Ariosto was killed before midnight. Well, we'd rented a bunch of videos which we watched till two in the morning. You can ask the desk clerk. He writes down the time you rent them and when you return them," Donna said. Then she smiled, recalling something. "That was also the night the VCR broke down and the guy had to come fix it. That must have been around eight or so, wasn't it, hon?"

"Yeah, it was," Sidney agreed. "He saw the both of us right here."

I believed them. "Why did Ariosto fire you?" I persisted.

"Why is that important?" Sidney asked.

"You've been around enough to know why." From his expression I could tell he knew it established motive. I also thought he was casting around swiftly for an answer.

"Well, as they said, the gin. Ariosto didn't need a reason to get rid of somebody. He chose the gin. It was as good as anything."

Sidney looked relieved that he'd hit on a reason that sounded plausible. I knew he was lying.

"That's all I'm going to say about it."

His fox-like features, sharp and in control, told me that he meant that. I wouldn't get anything else out of him. I gave him my card in case he had a change of heart. On a hunch I asked, "Did either one of you know Wilma Johnson? She worked at Tri State."

Both said they didn't know her.

I thanked them for their time and left.

Sidney had slipped up. Instead of confirming without hesitation that the theft of the Beefeater was the reason he got fired, he had initially denied it. Moreover, his denial rang truth. I was certain Ariosto hadn't fired him for something that paltry. What had been the real reason and why hide it? What was he trying to gain? A guy like Sidney never did anything without an eye toward profit.

On the way back to the office, I stopped at a Mobil station. While the attendant filled my tank, I reported my conversation with Sidney to Uncle Barney.

"I'm certain he knows something that has bearing on the murder, but he isn't going to spill it. At least not yet."

"What do you want to do? Call in Sam?"

"Sidney isn't going to tell Sam either. I know as sure as I'm standing here, the guy's hoping to profit from what he knows."

"Blackmail?"

"Or extortion." I could never remember the legal distinction between the two.

"You want me to put a tail on him and see whom he contacts?"

"Yes, but not yet. I don't think he's quite ready to pounce on his victim. He's not keyed up enough for that step."

"Good. Right now all the men are out. What's your next move, Cybil?"

"Make an appointment to see Ramsey Ariosto."

"Keep me posted."

I called Ramsey's secretary who put me right through. He was tied up the rest of the afternoon and most of the next day but could meet me for breakfast.

FOR OUR BREAKFAST MEETING I chose my good navy wool suit. To liven it up I selected a tailored shirt, slate-colored and slubbed with beige and navy stripes. I liked the shirt a lot but the silk-cotton combination fabric was a bear to iron.

The coffee shop of the downtown Holiday Inn was crowded, but Ramsey had reserved a booth where he was waiting for me, sipping coffee.

"Can we order right away?" he asked after shaking hands politely. "I have a meeting at nine-thirty."

"Sure. I only want coffee." Since I'd gotten up early, I'd already eaten a bowl of cereal with skim milk. I noticed that Ramsey studied me intently.

"You know, I remember you now. You knew Annette. Your name didn't ring a bell, but your face does. What I recall most vividly about you is your skin."

"My skin? How odd."

"Not really. The rest of us in high school bought benzoyl peroxide cream by the pound, but your skin was completely unblemished and clear. I envied you that flawless complexion. And you had long, long hair."

"Didn't we all?" I asked, smiling.

"Yeah." Ramsey smiled back, patting his thinning top.

"The reason I called you," I said after the waitress poured me a cup of coffee, "is because Annette hired me. She feels that you two are suspects in the murder of your uncle."

"I know. We discussed hiring you."

"Did you and your uncle have a fight?"

"Oh yeah. We had a humdinger of an argument Friday afternoon and no, I have no alibi for the time he was killed. The woman I was going to take to dinner Saturday night canceled. She'd come down with a bad cold. So, I spent the evening and the night alone in my apartment."

"Did anyone see you? Call you?"

"No."

"Did you order anything to be delivered? A pizza?"

He shook his head regretfully. "No, I popped a frozen pie in the oven. Believe me, if I'd known I'd need an alibi, I would have called Pizza Hut. As it was, I worked all evening on a report. Nobody even telephoned."

"What was the argument about between you and Mr. Ariosto?"

"Business. I wanted to change a procedure and he didn't. But it isn't…wasn't unusual for us to argue. Terrance had a confrontational personality. The only way for a man to keep from getting stomped into the ground was to yell back as loud as he yelled."

"You said for a man. What was the best way for women to get along with him?"

"Cater to him shamelessly. Flatter him. He was sharp enough to see through these tactics, of course, but he still enjoyed them."

"Is that what Pauline did?"

"Yes. At least at first. After she felt secure, she sloughed off but never enough to alienate Terrance. She's a clever and calculating woman where men are concerned."

"Annette thought the marriage was bound to fail. Do you agree?"

"Yeah. Terrance wasn't the long-term, faithful type.

He liked variety and change. But he was getting older which might have prolonged Pauline's tenure as his wife. Why are you asking about her?"

"If neither you nor Annette shot him, someone else did. I'm desperately looking for candidates. You care to nominate anyone?"

Ramsey wrinkled his forehead, his gray eyes thoughtful. At that moment I discerned a marked resemblance to his uncle.

"There is someone. Terrance and he have locked horns for years. Still…" Ramsey shook his head.

"Why now, right?"

He nodded.

"But something happened recently that could have heated up the conflict?" I guessed.

"Yup. You could say that. We were awarded a bid worth twenty-five million dollars in new construction."

"I didn't realized you were into building."

"Frontier Enterprises is an Ariosto subsidiary. One of our most profitable ventures."

I had seen many building sites marked by Frontier placards. "Whenever a big project is up for competitive bidding, somebody, several somebodies as a matter of fact, lose. They don't usually kill the winner. What happened?"

"Well, Alan Fettner, Terrance's arch rival, lost the bid to us by only a few thousand dollars. At the Rotary luncheon on Friday he and Terrance engaged in a shouting match which ended with them shoving each other until a couple of other Rotarians separated them."

I watched him carefully. I was certain he knew exactly what happened. "Okay. What happened? Why did they fight?"

"Accusations flew and one thing led to another."

"Ramsey, please don't make me drag this out of you. What you mean is that Fettner made accusations. About what?"

"Fixed bids."

"What made Fettner think that?"

Ramsey searched my eyes. I had the feeling he was weighing his words carefully.

"Fettner was paranoid. When he learned what our bid was, he hit the ceiling, telling everyone that Terrance had conspired to fix the bid. You see, the bid was only a little lower than his."

"How do you explain that?"

"We both figured the cost closely. We thought we could do it for what we entered. If you're going to fix a bid, it's less suspicious if you make the difference to the nearest bid bigger."

"He had no evidence? Just accused Frontier Enterprises of that?"

"Yes. Well, he hinted that the guy taking the bids was a friend of Terrance's who'd leaked the Fettner bid which was turned in ahead of ours."

"What was Ariosto's reaction?"

"First he said that if Fettner really believed that, he should bring charges against us. If not, he should shut up or we'd sue him for slander. That's when things really heated up and they got physical with each other."

"Do you know Fettner well?"

"Yes."

"Do you think he's capable of waiting for over twenty-four hours and then shooting your uncle?"

The waitress interrupted to serve breakfast, giving Ramsey a chance to think about his answer.

"I don't know. Fettner's got a temper, but I just don't know if he'd be capable of murder."

"How badly did losing this bid hurt him financially?"

"Nobody likes to lose a contract of that dimension. Still, I haven't heard any rumors that Fettner Enterprises is in trouble."

"How soon would you hear that sort of thing?"

"Pretty fast. At least rumors of trouble. Things like he was postdating checks to pay for supplies or taking out a loan, or being slow to meet his payroll. Those things leak quickly in a town our size."

"But you didn't hear anything like that?"

"No. Fettner did lose bids to us several times recently."

"Exactly how many and over what period of time?" I asked, pulling out a pad to make notes.

"Let me think. One in the spring and one last summer. And once before that. Maybe twenty months ago."

"That adds up to a lot of money."

"True. But we've lost bids, too. You figure for every three bids you make, you're doing great if you win one."

While Ramsey finished his eggs, I tried to decide what else to ask him. "Can you think of any other business competitors or of people who worked for your uncle who held a grudge against him?"

"Not the kind you murder for. Terrance wasn't liked

by people, but he paid well and that goes a long way to make up for bad manners and a hot temper."

"Even with you?"

He smiled at me. "Yes, even with me. Call it being perverse or something, but I liked the old pirate. We understood each other. Besides, he took a serious interest in me when my father died. He paid for me to get my MBA at Indiana University, taught me the business, and promoted me as I deserved it. He was also generous in his rewards. No, I had no reason to kill him."

"I know."

"Thank you, Cybil. I don't mean to look a gift horse in the mouth, but how do you know I didn't kill him?"

"You had no reason. Not a killing reason anyway. But most of all, you lost out financially with your uncle's death. I know about the shares you received for each year you worked for him."

"You're well informed."

"Do you know anyone in his personal life who would hate him enough to shoot him?" Again Ramsey chose his words with care.

"As I said, Terrance wasn't liked by many people. Not that he cared what people thought about him. I imagine it would have been easier to live with a hungry grizzly than him. But he was exceedingly generous and he could be charming when he set his mind to it."

He had to have been to accumulate four wives, not to mention a string of lady friends between marriages, I thought.

"What about Annette?" I asked.

"No way. She spent a lot of her life trying to win his approval. Or at least get his attention."

"How would he have felt if her marriage had broken up?"

"Are you speculating or do you know something?"

"Just answer my question, please."

"That would depend on the reason for the break up. If her husband had mistreated Annette, which I can't imagine, Terrance would have been the first to urge her to leave him. Any other reason…I don't know. Terrance was crazy about his grandchildren and proud of Annette's settled family life. I suspect in part because his own had been rather a mess. My guess is he would have been disappointed if her marriage had broken up."

I had been thinking of Sasha or whoever the man was she spent Saturday night with. Terrance would have disapproved of her infidelity, but that was no reason for her to shoot him. I was clutching at straws.

"Why are you asking me about Annette?"

I shrugged and changed the subject. "Have you been married?"

"Once. It didn't last. It was mostly my fault because I was too busy building a career to take the time to work on the relationship."

Ramsey was a nice guy, I thought. Not that nice guys don't occasionally kill someone. He could have gotten fed up with the constant arguments with Ariosto and his threats to fire him, brooded about it and…no, I couldn't buy that theory even as I formulated it.

"So, your prime candidate is Alan Fettner?" I asked.

He didn't look happy about that statement. "I'd hate to put it that strongly. Fettner's the only one who had a serious enough quarrel with my uncle recently. That's all I'm implying."

"Fair enough. Thanks for the coffee. May I call you if I have further questions?"

He said I could. He parted with a handshake in the parking lot.

At the agency I typed up a report on my meetings with Ramsey and Sidney. Then I reread everything in the Ariosto file, making notes of things to do. One of the items to pursue was the phone number listed among the travel brochures. Five minutes later I knew it wasn't a number used in the Westport area. Logic suggested that it had to be a number near Westport. Why would anyone call a travel agent halfway across the continent? What I had to do was take a map and draw ever widening circles around our town, prefix the various area codes to the number I had and place the calls. It sounded like a long, tedious job so I put it off till later.

The phone number reminded me of the mystery number I'd taken from behind Crawford's picture frame. Checking with Glenn, I learned that he'd struck out with all the possibilities we'd come up with. What could the blasted number be? More and more I leaned toward the notion that it was some kind of a code. If that was true, we'd probably never discover what it meant.

Discouraged, I looked at the next item on my list: the used glass on Ariosto's drink cart. If I took Sam to lunch would he tell me if they found prints on the glass? It was worth a try. He agreed pleasantly to meet me at the Casa Grande at noon. My treat.

NINE

SAM KELLER WAS IN THE BAR when I arrived at the Casa Grande. He finished his draft beer in one thirsty pull and joined me.

"Cousin, don't look so disapproving," he told me. "It's only on television that cops never drink while on duty. Besides, I don't consider one beer as drinking."

"I don't disapprove. Stop being so defensive."

Sam placed his hand against my back and nudged me in the direction of the dining room.

"I'm starved," he confessed. "The baby is teething and kept crying off and on all night. I overslept this morning and didn't get any breakfast."

"Not even a single donut?" I asked, knowing how addicted he is to sweet rolls.

"One donut doesn't count. A guy my size needs something more nourishing."

"How's Peggy?"

"Making noises about not waiting till the baby is two before she goes back to work. Claims her brain is turning into mush."

I smiled at the idea of Peggy's brain being anything but razor sharp. She's a first class accountant who does our taxes each spring.

"Do you need to look at the menu?" Sam asked as soon as the waitress appeared to pour water.

"No. We can order right away." For all his brave talk about drinking on duty, I noticed that he ordered coffee with his burrito.

"So, what is it that you want to know?"

I wasn't even tempted to pretend that this was anything but a business lunch. "Annette Ariosto Stevens hired me on advice from her attorney. They think that the police favor her or her cousin Ramsey as the murderer."

"Is that what they think?"

"How much truth is there to her suspicions?"

"Some. Neither has an alibi, and both gain financially." Sam raised his hand authoritatively to stop my rejoinder. "I know about the stock Ramsey gets each year. But he also gets a quarter of a million from the estate. That can buy a hell of a lot of stock."

"True, but I'm convinced that he didn't shoot Ariosto and neither did Ariosto's daughter. Have you found the murder weapon?"

"No. And not because we haven't tried."

"Any information about it?"

Sam told me about gauge and velocity and other technical things that didn't mean much to me.

"One thing's for sure. The shotgun as a choice of weapon indicates premeditation. Nobody walks around with a loaded shotgun. The killer went to Ariosto's loaded for bear."

I thought about that for a while. "There was no sign of forced entry, was there?"

"There wasn't."

"So, Ariosto must have let his killer in."

"Or he had a key."

Ignoring the implications of that, I said, "I can't picture Ariosto admitting the murderer into the house if
he was carrying a shotgun. The man wasn't a fool."

"It was raining, remember? The murderer could have
had the weapon hidden under his raincoat. Or he could
have used a sawed-off shotgun which can be carried
under a jacket."

"Then it could have been someone outside the family,"
I insisted.

"Anything's possible," Sam admitted but seemed
skeptical.

"Have you talked to the ex-chauffeur?"

Sam raised a pale golden eyebrow. "Should I have?
Why?"

I could have bitten off my tongue for mentioning it,
but I'd been sure Sam knew about it. "Ariosto fired him
on Friday."

"How did you find out about that?"

"From the staff." I wasn't about to mention names.

Scowling, Sam took out a small notebook. "Wait till
I talk to them again," he muttered.

"You can't blame them for not volunteering information to the police. Most of the time you guys aren't
exactly diplomatic or overly friendly."

"Name of the chauffeur," he demanded.

I told him, but revealed nothing else about Sidney.
The arrival of our food calmed Sam. Like most of the
Keller men, he loves to eat. While he attacked the huge,
cheese-covered burrito as though a seven-year famine
lurked outside the door, I picked at my taco salad.

"How about a little give and take," I suggested when

he paused for breath. "What about the used glass on the drink tray in the study?"

"No prints on it. The residue in it was gin and tonic."

"It couldn't have been Ariosto's drink since that was on his desk with some amber liquid in it."

"Scotch."

"He must have offered the murderer a drink."

"Or the killer poured himself a gin and tonic afterwards."

I shuddered at the idea of anyone cold enough to fix a drink while the body was lying a few feet away, bleeding and still warm. "Any prints on the decanters?"

Sam nodded. "Ariosto's and the butler's."

Summing up, I said, "What we have here is a murderer who drinks gin and tonic. The glass had to be his. Nobody else would wipe off their prints. It's someone Ariosto knew, and it's a man."

"Why a man?"

"The shotgun. It's such a…my feminist friends will disown me for saying this, but it's such a masculine weapon. Big. Unwieldy. Loud. It's a gut reaction, nothing more," I admitted.

"I have the same gut reaction. Physically a shotgun is unwieldy, especially if it has to be hidden against the body of the person carrying it."

"Did you find anything else in the study? Something that shouldn't have been there?"

"You know I can't reveal anything specific." Pushing his empty plate away, Sam lit a cigarette.

"But you can answer with a yes or a no, right?"

"Maybe. Depends on the question."

"Did you find any fingerprints you can't account for?"

"No."

"Anything under Ariosto's fingernails?"

"No. He was shot at close range but the murderer wasn't close enough for Ariosto to grab him while falling."

"I picture the killer standing by the decanter, his back toward Ariosto. He takes the shotgun out from under his raincoat, turns and shoots."

Sam nodded. "He probably took a couple of steps toward Ariosto before he let him have it."

"Can you put a face on the murderer?"

"No. But that's off the record. Can you?"

"No. I wish I could."

"Is that enough give or take?"

"Yes, thank you. Unless you want to volunteer something?"

Sam ignored that. Pushing back the sleeve of his navy blazer, he glanced at his watch. "Cybil, I hate to eat and run, but I've got to be at the courthouse in thirty minutes."

"That's okay. Go ahead. I'll have another cup of coffee."

"Thanks for lunch. Be careful, Cybil. This is murder. That raises the ante considerably."

"I'm always careful."

I asked the waitress for a refill and the check. Somehow I had to get in to see Fettner. I was fairly sure he wouldn't agree to see me if I telephoned for an appointment. Ramsey had given me a good description of the man as well as his business and home address.

Deciding to try a long shot, I drove to his business. The offices took up the entire, flat-roofed building. I parked so that I could see the reserved executive parking spaces. Fortunately, they all seemed to be still out to lunch or away on a construction site. I took the copy of my latest hatha yoga magazine and flipped through it. As much as I wanted to read it cover to cover, I didn't dare, knowing how caught up I get. If it's something interesting, the whole world could pass by and I wouldn't notice.

A white BMW arrived. The driver parked in a reserved spot. Unfortunately, of the four men who got out none was Fettner. They were too short and not nattily enough dressed to fit his description. Slowly all the spaces filled but one. Fettner didn't arrive at the office until three o'clock. By then I had shifted my body into every position permitted by the car seat, had balanced my checkbook, had finished the crossword puzzle in the *Chicago Tribune,* and had studied the wallpaper swatches long enough to have picked the one I wanted for the dining room. I wrote down Fettner's license plate number as Uncle Barney insists we do just in case we'll need it.

Since the only clue I could work on in the office consisted of tracing the phone number, I lingered in the parking lot, speculating that since Fettner, who'd arrived carrying a hard hat, might have worked through lunch and might take off early. He did, a few minutes later, having exchanged his dark gray suit for tailored cords, a sweater whose V-neck was filled by an ascot tie and a wind breaker with a famous logo on the pocket. I followed his black Lincoln at a discreet distance.

Fifteen minutes later we arrived at the Riverview Country Club. Fettner took a golf bag from his trunk, checked his watch, and sauntered inside. From his pace I figured he was early and this was as good a time as any to talk to him. Being a Riverview member, I strolled right in.

My quarry was at the bar, ordering a drink. When I sat down on the stool beside him, he looked at me, surprised. His surprise changed to pleasure. Seeing his dove-gray sweater up close, I knew it was cashmere.

"Can I buy you a drink?" he asked in a low, coaxing voice when the bartender placed a Bloody Mary in front of him.

"Thank you. I'll have one of those," I said, indicating the tomato juice concoction, "but without the vodka."

"A virgin one, huh?" he asked, amused.

Since I wanted information from him, I decided to be friendly. I smiled. We introduced ourselves.

"You're a builder, aren't you?" I asked, all but batting my eyelashes at him.

"Why, yes," he said, pleased. "How did you know that?"

"Don't be so modest. Your company's signs are all over the county. Yours and Frontier's are practically on every construction site in the city. Is Frontier your biggest competitor?"

"It was. I don't know what'll happen in the future."

Pretending to remember, I said, "That's right. The owner of Frontier was shot last Saturday night. Ariosto was his name, wasn't it?"

"Yes, God rest his soul."

His pious sentiment struck a wrong note.

"You knew him?"

"Sure. For years."

"Isn't that something, him getting shot like that?"

"Probably some hopped up drug addict looking for something to steal." He downed a third of the good-sized Bloody Mary.

"But the paper said robbery wasn't a motive. It could have been an angry competitor."

That startled him. "That's a hell of an idea. If every angry businessman killed his competitor that would put an end fast to free enterprise as we know it." Staring at me hard, Fettner added, "You didn't just drop in for a friendly drink, did you?"

"No. I followed you."

"Who are you?" His eyes narrowed suspiciously.

I told him.

Considerably less friendly than before, he asked, "What do you want?"

"I understand you leveled serious accusations against Ariosto before the two of you indulged in a shoving match at last Friday's Rotary luncheon."

"So what? That doesn't mean I shot him the next day."

"No, but I would like to make certain you have an alibi. I have to rule out suspects or add them to my list. Where were you Saturday evening between seven and eight?"

"I don't have to tell you that."

"True. But then the police will be here to ask you that before you can tee off." That wiped the belligerent expression off his face.

"I have nothing to hide from anybody except my wife."

"I'm discreet. It's a prerequisite of my job."

"I won't deny that I was ticked off at Ariosto. But that wasn't so much because he underbid me by a few lousy bucks, but because he gloated over it. He had to rub my nose in it. Ariosto may have been a good businessman and he may have pulled himself up by his bootstraps financially, but socially he never left the gutter he grew up in. He was boorish, ill-mannered, crude and profane." Picking up the small cocktail napkin, Fettner patted his mouth with a precise, fastidious gesture.

I didn't think there were more than two or three people who would disagree with that assessment of Ariosto.

"That still doesn't tell me where you were Saturday evening when he was killed."

"I was right here. Not in the bar but in one of the private rooms."

That surprised me. Fettner seemed too refined to partake of the profanity-laced, smoke-filled, high-stakes poker games that take place in the private rooms on weekends.

"My wife is violently opposed to any kind of gambling, but I enjoy a good game of baccarat once in a while."

Baccarat. Of course. How could I have ever suspected him of anything as vulgar as five-card stud?

"Can anyone verify that?"

"Baccarat's scarcely a game you play by yourself," he informed me, just a trifle condescendingly. Calling to the bartender, Fettner asked, "Is Lou here yet?"

"No. He won't be in till five."

"Lou was the dealer that night."

Several men entered the bar. Fettner motioned to one of them to join us. "Kirby, where did you see me Saturday night?"

"Right here," Kirby answered, looking at me with undisguised curiosity.

"Here in the bar?" I asked.

"Yeah, and elsewhere," Kirby said, trying to guess how much he should reveal.

"Kirby, tell her exactly where we were between seven and eleven."

"In room 117, playing cards."

"Thanks, Kirby."

Dismissed by Fettner, Kirby joined his friends.

"This better not get back to my wife."

"It won't. Thanks for your time." Placing a five dollar bill on the bar for the jazzed up tomato juice, I left.

AT THE OFFICE I TRIED to trace the phone number by dialing various area codes first. After thirty minutes I decided there had to be a more logical way to proceed. If for some reason I didn't want to use a local travel agency, where would I go? To a large city. Using this theory I dialed the area code for Indianapolis and the number. A recorded male voice informed me that I had reached the True Church of the Light whose shepherd was out at the moment. The voice blessed me mechanically before inviting me to leave a message.

In Chicago, which I realized in retrospect was the city I should have called first, I reached the A-Z Travel Agency. Pretending to double check arrangements for the Ariostos, I found out that Mr. and Mrs. Ariosto had reservations on the S.S. Oslo for a Caribbean cruise starting December 27th. Interesting, I thought, but didn't see how that helped me clear Annette of suspicion. As a matter of fact, at that moment I had absolutely no idea what to do next to clear her.

Since I always think better when I walk, I grabbed my coat and set out for a prowl through the historic section of the city that adjoins the downtown area. The cobblestone streets, gaslights and big, old houses appeal to me. I had wanted to buy a house here but Luke wouldn't hear of it. These houses, he claimed, were impossible to heat in our near-arctic winters. Not only that, they needed continuous repair. So, when we separated, I bought an old house in the area.

I wanted a house that was as different from the suburban home I'd shared with my little boy as I could find. The familiar ache settled on my chest, making breathing difficult. Maxi assures me that one day the memory will hurt less, but I wonder. I walked fast, as if my pace could outrun the pain. It couldn't, of course. After a while I turned around and went back to the office.

"Where have you been?" Lynn demanded, pouncing on me the moment I walked back into the agency.

I glanced at my watch. "I've only been gone twenty-five minutes."

"It doesn't look good for the agency if the police are always camping on our doorstep."

I looked around pointedly. "The police?"

"One Sergeant Griffin. I put him in the small conference room. He says he won't leave without you. What have you done now?"

She made it sound as if I were a habitual offender. "What does he say I've done?"

"He doesn't. 'It's routine'," she mimicked.

Ah. Lynn was as upset by the inspector's refusal to confide in her as she was by his presence. She loves being privy to all that's going on.

"Are you sure you don't know what he wants?"

"Would I lie to you?" I gazed at her as guilelessly as I could manage.

She looked at me, uncertain whether I was serious or facetious. "I guess I'd better go and face the music."

As I entered the conference room, a series of sneezes greeted me. "Gesundheit."

Sergeant Griffin's face appeared from behind a large crumpled handkerchief. "Thank you." Rising from the straight-backed chair he'd been sitting on, he said, "Mrs. Quindt, Lieutenant Keller wants to see you."

"That's what Lynn told me. When?"

"Now." His cocker spaniel eyes looked apologetic.

"This very minute?"

"Yes, ma'am. I'm not to return to the station without you."

Sergeant Griffin's long, perpetually melancholy face didn't look too happy at the possibility of having to drag me against my will to the police station. "Why does the lieutenant want to see me?"

"It's routine."

"That's such a convenient phrase. Covers everything, doesn't it?" I smiled at him, adding to his discomfort.

Marching past Lynn with my police escort, I said, "You will inform Uncle Barney of my trip to the police station when he gets back, okay? And get the bail money ready, just in case." I saw an alarmed expression settle on her face.

The sergeant escorted me to an unmarked sedan.

"Sergeant, that can't be a cold," I said after he had sneezed his way to the driver's side of the car. "What are you allergic to?"

He made a dismissing gesture with his hand. "What aren't I allergic to, that's the question. My doctor says that in twenty years of practicing medicine he hasn't seen a case worse than mine," Griffin said, clearly proud of that distinction.

It always amazes me that people love the superlative even if it pertains to something bad. "What are you doing for it?"

"Everything." During the short trip to the station, he recited the highlights of his complicated health regimen. Then he escorted me to Sam's cubicle in the upstairs squad room.

"Mrs. Quindt," he announced with a gravity that would have done an imperial herald proud.

"Thank you, Griffin." Sam fixed me with cool, blue eyes. "Have a seat, Cybil."

I sat. When the sergeant positioned himself behind me, notebook in hand, I knew this was an official occasion.

"When was the last time you saw Sidney Dunn?" Sam asked.

"Day before yesterday."

"Where did you see him?"

"At the Airport Inn." That rated a surprised stare.

"I'll probably regret asking, but how did you locate him there?"

"Brilliant deductive reasoning." Sam was about to snap at me for that but controlled himself. "Are you looking for him?"

"Not anymore."

I didn't like the sound of that. "You found him?"

"Yes."

Getting answers from Sam could be like quizzing a brick wall. Sam was in one of his famous stubborn Keller moods. I tried a different approach. "Since you've found Sidney, why do you want to talk with me? He can tell you anything you want to know."

"I wish that were true," Sam mumbled.

"Sam, don't be cryptic. It's not your style. What's going on? Either tell me or charge me with something or I'm leaving."

"What did you and Sidney talk about at the Airport Inn? Does Luke know you went to that sleazy place?"

"What my husband knows or doesn't know is beside the point!"

"Temper, temper, Cybil. I repeat what did you and Sidney talk about?"

I took two deep, calming breaths before I answered. "We discussed the reasons for him getting fired."

"Which were?"

"I don't know. Sidney implied it was over the theft of a case of gin, but he wasn't telling the truth. Or at least not all of it."

Sam sat, waiting for me to explain further. "I thought he knew something about Ariosto's murder that he wasn't saying. I had a hunch he might try to raise money with that knowledge."

"Blackmail?"

"That's how I read the situation. Sam, what happened?"

"Dunn's dead. Shot like Ariosto and Crawford."

"Oh, my God."

"A glass of water, sergeant," Sam yelled.

"I'm okay," I managed to say. "I should have asked Uncle Barney to put him under surveillance. If I had, Sidney Dunn might be alive today."

"Maybe and maybe not. Even if we'd pulled him in for questioning, there's no guarantee that he'd have come clean. He probably would have attempted the blackmail anyway and wound up just as dead. Don't blame yourself."

"Drink this," the sergeant said, pressing a paper cup into my hands. Dutifully I sipped some.

"If you feel faint, put your head down between your knees," the sergeant advised.

"I'm not going to faint. I never faint. Sam, where did you find Sidney's body?"

"In his apartment."

"Did his landlady call you?"

"Yeah. She was coming home from the grocery store when she saw the upstairs lights on. She hadn't seen him for several days so she went up."

"Have you notified his girlfriend?"

"Donna Clark? Yes."

"Poor woman."

"How do you know her?"

"From the motel. She was there."

"You do get around. Any idea what Sidney held back?"

I shook my head. "He drove Ariosto as well as other

members of the household. Obviously he saw or heard something that pointed to the murderer. Or to someone else who could be embarrassed if that piece of information came out. Unlike Brazier and Mrs. Dougherty, Sidney didn't feel as loyal as they did."

"Anything else you have forgotten to mention? Any little old thing?"

Usually I'm impervious to Sam's heavy-handed sarcasm, but I was feeling burdened with guilt about Sidney, so I told him about my conversation with Alan Fettner. I couldn't handle another murder that I might have prevented if I'd done something.

"I'm going to have another talk with everybody connected with this case." Anger threaded Sam's voice.

"Try the polite approach. It gets more answers than your abrasive manner," I advised.

"Thank you, Miss Manners. You may go."

He didn't have to give me permission twice. I practically shot out of my chair. At the door I paused. "I remember something else," I said. "Sidney was hiding out from his ex-wife."

"Thank you for sharing this. Is there anything else that conveniently slipped your mind?"

"No."

"Cybil, the count's up to three murders. I hope you're telling me all you know."

I didn't care for the threat in Sam's voice but I managed to answer calmly. "I am. Honestly. But the count's up to four. Don't forget Wilma." Sam waved his hand dismissively. "Can I have Donna's address? I'd like to send her a condolence note. She was in love with Sidney."

Sam hesitated.

"Oh, for heaven's sake! The woman must be devastated. I only want to do the decent thing."

Grudgingly he supplied it with the caution, "But if she lets anything slip that seems pertinent, I expect you to pass it on. Promise, Cybil."

"I promise."

I walked back to the agency. Since Uncle Barney wasn't back yet, I drove home. Too restless and agitated to think clearly and productively, I decided to join my hatha yoga group. That decision made, I flung off my suit, pulled on silver-gray tights, a mauve leotard, sneakers and jeans and took off again.

Two hours later I emerged feeling tranquil and at one with the universe. The harmonious mood stayed with me while I stir-fried vegetables and tofu for my dinner. Hatha yoga classes always inspire me to embrace an innocent vegetarian diet.

The phone rang. A woman's voice spoke to me, but it was difficult to understand the words because she was sobbing.

TEN

"DONNA?" I ASKED, guessing her identity.

"I'm sorry. I thought I was done crying for a while." She broke off, sobbing again.

"That's okay." Donna's raw pain tore at me.

"Have you heard about Sidney?"

"Yes, and I'm sorry. Can I do anything for you?"

"That's why I called. Sidney left an envelope I'm supposed to give to you."

For an instant I was speechless with surprise. "Donna, do you know what's in the envelope?"

"No. It's sealed. Sidney said to call you right away if...if anything happened to him."

"How awful for you. Do you have someone who can stay with you?"

"My sister is on her way."

"Do you have a doctor?"

"No."

"I'll be over as fast as I can." I hung up. Then I called Luke to ask if there was anything I could give Donna to calm her down.

"I can't prescribe anything for her without having examined her. Give her chamomile tea with honey. It has a mild sedative effect. Offer her sympathy. Listen to her. You're good at that."

"Luke, if she's completely falling apart, may I call you again?"

He sighed. "Yes. Even after seven years of marriage I have a hard time resisting your pleas. Maybe because you only plead for others and never for yourself."

"Thank you, Luke."

DONNA LIVED IN THE southern part of the city. I drove around for fifteen frustrating minutes looking for her street. This was the oldest subdivision in the city where the only logic visible in laying out the streets was the use of Indian tribes in naming them. Kickapoo was a one-block street between Apache and Huron. Indians of the Great Plains, the New England woodlands and the Southwest were placed cheek-by-jowl, so not even the names adhered to any kind of order. Disgusted by the unnecessary delay, I muttered a few uncomplimentary things about city planners.

The house was a tiny square box, distinguished from its neighbors by the flower box under the picture window which was filled with plastic pink geraniums. Donna opened the door. Her eyes were nearly swollen shut from the tears which were still pouring down her face. I couldn't help but hug her. Feeling the agony of her loss, the memory of mine threatened to break through. I fought my tears hard.

After a few seconds, Donna gained control over her weeping. With a soggy tissue pressed against her face, she asked me to come in.

"How soon do you expect your sister?" I asked.

"Any time now. She had to get the kids ready to bring them along. I guess they'll all spend the night."

"That's good. You shouldn't be alone."

Donna nodded. Apparently remembering why I was there, she picked up an envelope from the coffee table.

"Sidney gave me this right after you spoke to us on Tuesday."

"Thank you." Eagerly I ripped it open. The business-sized envelope contained a key with a plastic tag attached to it. The lettering on the tag, which had been originally golden, was mostly rubbed off. I took the key to the lamp on the end table. Even though the bulb wasn't overly bright, I managed to decipher the printing. "The Dolphin #18," I read aloud. "Does that mean anything to you?"

Donna shook her head. "When I went to Florida, we stayed in a motel by that name but that was four years before I met Sidney. There couldn't be a connection."

"I agree. What exactly did Sidney say when he gave you the envelope? Think, Donna. It's important."

"He said, 'Give this to Mrs. Quindt if anything happen to me.' I asked him what he thought might happen to him. He laughed and hugged me but told me nothing. Just gave me a flip answer like in case his car went down into the river or something like that, I should call you. I begged him to stop what he was doing but he wouldn't. He said we deserved something, that he was tired of other people having everything."

"Do you know what he was up to?"

"No. He just said that soon we'd be living on easy street. No more kowtowing to rich people. He knew something that was worth a lot of money. I told him

I didn't want the money if he could get hurt, but he wouldn't listen."

"Did Sidney know a lot of rich people beside the Ariosto family?"

"I don't think so."

Just as I suspected. Sidney had something on one of the family members.

"Mrs. Quindt, all I ever wanted was Sidney. Maybe he didn't look like much to you, but he was good to me. He never hit me. He never even yelled or lost his temper. And he didn't get falling down drunk or do drugs. He was kind and gentle and…." Donna started to cry again.

"When did he leave today?"

"At six when I went to work. He took me. I do the breakfast shift at the Pancake Shoppe. I didn't see him again. The cops arrived right after I got home. I still can't believe Sidney isn't going to walk through that door."

She sobbed harder now. I sat on the couch beside her. Placing my arm around her shoulder I murmured comforting things. Eventually she calmed down enough for me to ask her more questions.

"Did he talk about Mr. Ariosto's murder?"

"We heard it on the Saturday evening news. Sunday morning Sidney got up early to buy the newspaper. He sort of chuckled after he'd read the article about the murder. He said something like 'for two cents I'd call the cops and tell 'em what I know.' Then he got that funny look on his face. He winked at me and said, 'I know how we'll come into a lot of easy money, babe.

No more driving for me, and no more hash slinging for you.' Does that help?"

"Some. He never said anything specific? Like from whom he was going to get this money?"

"No." Donna shook her head.

"Were you together the whole time since Saturday?"

"Yeah. Except when I was working. I had Tuesday off. Sidney didn't want to stay at his place because his ex-wife was bugging him about back alimony and my daughter was home that day. That's why we were at the motel," she explained.

"When you two were here, did he ever go out alone?"

"Yes. On Monday."

"Did he say where he was going?"

"No. Just said to wish him luck." Donna thought for a moment. "Wait. After he'd gone I went into the kitchen to start dinner and that's when I put the stuff away he'd left on the kitchen table. He'd been looking at a map of the university. I couldn't figure out why."

"A map of the buildings on campus?"

Donna nodded.

Crawford had driven to campus with me tailing him to the Alpha House complex. Sidney, contemplating blackmail, studied a map of the university. This was too odd to be a coincidence.

The doorbell rang, followed by a female voice calling Donna.

"That's my sister."

Donna opened the door and threw herself at a

younger woman loaded down with blankets, pillows and a teddy bear.

"It's going to be okay, sis," the newcomer said. "I'm here. Come on in, kids, and close the door," she yelled behind her.

I tried not to look at the children, but, of course, I did. One appeared to be six. The other, too bundled up to give a clue to its sex, was younger. Perhaps four, the age my Ryan would be had he lived. One of my secret fears is that some day a mother is going to light into me, suspecting me of God knows what because I look at her child with hungry eyes. Switching my gaze to the women, I saw that Donna's sister was the take-charge type. Relieved, I bid the women goodbye and left.

I PHONED UNCLE BARNEY who asked me to report verbatim which I did, having a fairly good memory. He does that when he wants to get the underlying nuances of an interview.

"I'm fairly certain Sam doesn't suspect me of the Dunn killing," I concluded. "Sorry I didn't call sooner, but Donna's really broken up. From what she says, she tried to stop Sidney from going after the easy money, but he wouldn't listen. If only I had asked you to put him under surveillance he might still be alive."

"I doubt that. Cybil, if he was set on blackmail he would have proceeded with it no matter what, and that's a dangerous crime. If you want to keep on doing this kind of work and not develop ulcers, you'll have to stop taking on the guilt of the world."

"I know."

"Tell me what Donna had to say."

"All she knows is that Sidney studied a map of the campus and left an envelope for me in case something happened to him. The envelope contained a key attached to a plastic tag engraved with The Dolphin #18."

"What does the key look like?"

"It reminds me of the kind motels and hotels used to have."

"What are you planning to do with it?"

"First thing in the morning I'm going to the main branch of the public library and start checking their telephone directories for hotels and motels. I'll start with the towns closest to Westport and work out from there. There can't be that many places in the Midwest named The Dolphin."

"Let me know what you find out."

"I will," I promised before I hung up.

I took a shower. Wrapped in a pink fleece robe I looked through the television offerings. An old movie with Melina Mercouri caught my eye. This reminded me of the first time I saw Luke. It was at a campus film festival. I think I fell in love with him when we discussed one of those heavily symbolic Ingmar Bergman films over coffee in the student union. Sometimes that seems a lifetime ago.

While I was waiting for the movie to start, I wondered if I really would be satisfied with merely clearing Annette. Deep down I wanted the murderer caught, justice done, and order restored. And I had to admit to myself that I would be happy if I could help bring about these things.

THE WESTPORT PUBLIC LIBRARY had celebrated its hundredth year and had outgrown the present facility some time ago. The out-of-town telephone directories stood tightly wedged behind the computerized card catalogue. I worked with them there, seated in a comfortable chair, until the smell of unwashed bodies and dirty clothes drove me to a far corner table. With cold weather settling in, the library became a favorite place of the homeless.

After checking all the towns within a hundred-mile radius, I found one motel named The Dolphin. Quite logically it was located near Lake Michigan.

My next step was to drive to The Dolphin and take a look at it. Since it was a sunny fall day, I decided to drive north before turning west on Michigan State Road 12. It's a lovely drive. My only regret was that the trees had already lost their colorful fall foliage.

After expecting the place to be more on the order of the Airport Inn, The Dolphin was a pleasant surprise. The swing set in the play area indicated that this was a family-oriented establishment, so what connection could it have with murder?

Before I did anything else I had to find out if the key fit the lock to Room 18. The parking space in front of that room was empty. Gambling that the occupant had left by now, I walked to the door, knocked and announced, "Maid service." When no one answered, I tried the key. It unlocked the door smoothly, silently.

The room had either been made up already or it hadn't been rented the night before. Still, I decided to check to see if anything had been left behind. The wastepaper basket in the bathroom was empty, as were the dresser drawers and the closet. I closed the door and returned to my car where I sat for a while trying to guess the significance of Sidney's clue. Since I couldn't solve the puzzle, I returned to the agency.

Uncle Barney was having lunch with a client. That gave me time to think some more about the key. Obviously Sidney had believed that I would be able to come up with the right solution or he wouldn't have left it for me. The only thing vaguely useful that popped into my mind was to stake out Room 18 and see what happened.

Surprisingly, Uncle Barney agreed with my plan when I broached it. He assigned me the eight to midnight watch. That way I could attend Terrance Ariosto's funeral which was scheduled for two o'clock that afternoon. I came close to pleading with him to send someone else, but managed to restrain myself. He obviously thought I could handle going to the funeral. I couldn't disappoint him.

Since wearing slacks to such a solemn event seemed tacky, I hurried home to change into a full-skirted, loden green wool suit with a large matching fringed shawl and brown dress boots. My attendance served a dual purpose: I represented the agency in paying our respects, and more prosaically, I was there "to note who else was attending," as Uncle Barney put it. Not that any of us believe that a lightning bolt would strike the murderer at the grave site. Still, it wouldn't hurt to observe reactions and expressions.

The closer I got to the cemetery, the shakier I felt. When Uncle Barney asked me to attend the funeral I agreed because I wanted to prove to myself that I could do this without falling apart. My horror of funerals goes as far back as I can remember. I'm told that as a four-year-old attending my father's burial, I screamed when his coffin was lowered into the ground. Perhaps that explains my unreasonable fear of shut-up, dark or small places like elevators, cellars, and rooms without windows. What going through a long tunnel does to me is difficult for anyone untroubled by claustrophobia to understand. Having to place my sweet son's body into the cold earth did nothing to decrease my terror of funerals.

Suddenly deeply buried memories burst through the surface of my consciousness. I felt my heart skip a beat, then kick into a fast, hard rhythm that was as painful as it was scary. My breathing grew shallow and rapid. I felt as if I couldn't get enough air. I pulled into the cemetery parking lot, my hands frozen on the steering wheel. I couldn't move. *Breathe deeply, slowly,* my mind urged, not yet completely overtaken by panic and anxiety.

Closing my eyes, I envisioned my hatha yoga teacher and heard her say, "Breathe in to the count of four, hold, and breathe out to the count of eight." Doing this, I stopped myself from hyperventilating. By the time I had conquered my anxiety and could breathe normally, perspiration dotted my forehead. Several minutes later I was able to get out of the car. Though my legs felt weak, I was able to follow the mourners to the grave.

Standing to one side, I watched the family members arrive and be seated on the folding chairs arranged for them. Annette, wearing a beige cape trimmed with rich brown fur, undoubtedly mink, irritably brushed aside the solicitous hand of a black-clad attendant holding a chair for her. Her banker husband appeared self-assured and trust-inspiring even as he contemplated the copper casket. In direct contrast, Harry looked absurdly vulnerable, young, and uncertain. My heart went out to him. He waited until his stepmother took her seat before he hunched down into his.

Pauline drew the magnificent black, full-length fur coat around herself, whether for warmth or psychological protection, I wasn't sure. I was sure, however, that the sunglasses she wore didn't hide tear-swollen eyes. No emotion was visible on her face except a slight defiance as if she dared anyone approach her for not pretending to be grief-stricken. The only tears I saw shed at the service coursed down Mrs. Dougherty's broad, kind face.

Listening to the minister read the Twenty-Third Psalm, I dug my fingernails into the palms of my hands to retain control. Mercifully the service was brief.

Ramsey Ariosto caught up with me on my way to the parking lot. He relayed Annette's invitation to join them for a drink at the house. Although I wasn't in the mood to socialize, I reminded myself that as an investigator I might garner something that would shed light on the three murders that had us baffled.

I took my time getting to the Ariosto mansion, giving the family a chance to get ready for the reception—if that was the right word for the occasion. Wake implied camaraderie and conviviality, neither of which I expected to find at the mansion.

Brazier, even more solemn-faced than usual, opened the door and took my shawl. I waited my turn to go through the receiving line, murmuring condolences. The only ones who seemed to need them were Annette and Harry. The former was pale under the blush that sat prominently on her gaunt cheeks and the dark circles under her eyes no amount of makeup could conceal; the latter's handsome face was ashen, the blue eyes constantly darting from one object to another, searching for…I had the disquieting feeling that not even Harry knew what he hoped to find.

In the dining room a lavish buffet was spread out on the long table. Even though I had skipped lunch, I couldn't bring myself to take food. Instead I accepted a glass of orange juice without gin from the young man behind the bar which was set up in a corner of the room.

Since Annette had murmured to me that we needed to talk, I had to wait until her hostess' duties were done. Not feeling like making small talk with people I didn't know, I went to the kitchen where I saw two women replenish trays of food. Since Mrs. Dougherty wasn't one of them, I went to the servants' sitting room.

"May I come in?" I asked her.

"Oh sure. I'd be glad of the company," Mrs. Dougherty said. "Come and have some of this food. It's catered, so I can't guarantee its quality."

On the coffee table sat a tray of assorted, small sandwiches, chicken wings, shrimp and relishes. I watched her pick up a sandwich, look at it critically, and take a bite.

"Just as I thought. They used store-bought bread. For what they charge they could at least get bakery bread."

"Any cucumber sandwiches among those?"

"No, but I'll fix us some."

Before I could request for her not to go to any trouble,

she'd gone. She came back within minutes, carrying a chopping block, a golden loaf of homemade bread, mayonnaise, a pepper mill and a long, English cucumber. I watched her skilled hands assemble four cucumber sandwiches, two of which she put on a plate for me.

I thanked her, suddenly discovering that I was hollow with hunger. Between bites I asked her about her plans for the future.

"Mr. Ariosto, God rest his soul, set up a pension plan for me years ago. I think I'll retire and do some volunteer work in the community. Brazier's retiring, too, so I don't know what Miss Annette will do with the house."

"What about Mrs. Ariosto?"

"Her?" Mrs. Dougherty shrugged. "She gets a generous allowance each month. My guess is that she'll spend it in Chicago or New York among the bright lights and excitement. She never liked Westport. Always complained that there was nothing to do here."

"She seems to be holding up well."

Mrs. Dougherty uttered a sound that was a cross between a snort and a sniff and all pure contempt.

"Why shouldn't she hold up well? It isn't as if she'd been crazy in love with her husband. Her kind rarely is."

"Was she in love with someone else?"

Mrs. Dougherty eyed me shrewdly. "She might have been. Something's the matter with her, that's for sure. She doesn't act like herself."

"How does she act?"

"Skittish. Drops things when you walk up behind her. Drinks way too much."

"It's only natural that her husband's murder would upset her."

"It started before that."

"Oh? How long ago?"

Mrs. Dougherty thought for a minute. "It's hard to pinpoint exactly when someone starts to change, but I think it happened this summer. Some days she'd be real up and happy. Other's she'd snap and bite your head off for no reason. Sometimes I suspected she'd been crying and she's not the crying type."

"How had Pauline acted before this summer?"

"Sort of lady-of-the-manor like. She enjoyed giving orders and being waited on."

"And Mr. Ariosto? How did he treat her?"

Mrs. Dougherty shrugged. "The way he treated all his wives."

In other words, abominably, I thought. "Did he notice the change in her?"

"He noticed the drinking, and he didn't like it. I don't know if he was aware of anything else."

From the way she said this, I knew she wouldn't elaborate.

We finished our sandwiches in silence.

"Harry doesn't look well. Have you noticed that?" I asked after a while.

"My poor lamb. He doesn't eat much even when I fix his favorite foods, and I suspect he sleeps even less. I would never have thought his stepfather's death would hit him so hard. But then Mr. Ariosto was the only family he had left since his mother passed away. Poor boy."

"I talked to Sidney shortly before he was killed," I began but Mrs. Dougherty interrupted.

"Wasn't that just awful? I can't believe what's going on out there. Poor Sidney."

"He told his lady friend that he was going to come into big money. Sidney suggested it was going to come from someone in this house. Do you know what he was hinting at?"

"Sidney was always talking about making it big. I can't remember how many times he sat at my kitchen table, filling in a racing form or studying the winning lottery numbers. Each time he placed a bet he was sure he'd win a bundle. I wouldn't put any store in anything Sidney said about coming into money. Nothing but wishful thinking, if you ask me."

Brazier interrupted us to tell me that Annette was ready to see me in the morning room.

"Have you found out anything?" she demanded as soon as I crossed the threshold.

Sensing her agitation, I answered from the doorway. "Yes, we've learned several things, but they're not conclusive. We're still working on our leads."

Annette sucked on her cigarette almost fiercely, dragging the smoke deep into her lungs.

"Where were you yesterday around noon?" I asked. Since she didn't believe in beating around the bush, I didn't either.

Annette peered at me through the smoke drifting from her cigarette. "Why?"

"The police will ask you that, probably before the day is out." She didn't look happy at the prospect. For a beat I thought she was going to refuse to answer my question.

"I went to the funeral home to make sure everything was in order. Then I met my husband at the airport. He came in on the noon flight from Detroit."

"Good."

"Cybil, I insist on knowing why I need an alibi."

"Sidney Dunn was shot around noon. His head was practically blown off with a shotgun."

Behind me I heard something that sounded like someone gagging. I turned in time to see Pauline running into the downstairs powder room.

ELEVEN

ANNETTE JOINED ME IN TIME to see her father's widow run into the bathroom. Our eyes met. She raised an eyebrow and shrugged one elegant shoulder.

"Pauline was perfectly composed during the funeral and the reception, so why should news of the chauffeur's death upset her?" Annette wondered.

I wondered, too. If Pauline had shot Sidney, she would have prepared herself to receive the news of his death with the correct mixture of polite shock, horror and surprise. But if Sidney had been blackmailing her and somebody else had killed him, Pauline's natural reaction would be one of relief. For her to become physically ill made no sense. But it was interesting, interesting enough for me to pursue further. Turning to Annette, I asked, "How long have you had seats in Orchestra Hall?"

"We've had season tickets for twenty years or more. I think Dad's first wife was a music lover. I suspect she's the one who started the subscription."

"Are the seats the same ones each year?"

"Yes. For as long as I can remember we've had two seats in the twelfth row. Why do you ask?"

"No special reason," I murmured.

Annette went back into the morning room, crushed her cigarette in an ashtray and immediately lit another. I lingered in the doorway long enough to see Pauline drag herself upstairs, white-faced and ill-looking. As soon as I decently could, I left Annette with assurances of informing her of my progress.

I went into the kitchen where the same caterer's employees fixed sandwiches. Neither woman objected when I put the kettle on and prepared a tray. When the tea had steeped, I carried the tray upstairs. Assuming that the master suite was still in the same location, I knocked on its door.

"Go away."

Pauline's voice sounded muffled. "I brought you some tea. I'm coming in." Before she could object, I opened the door. The sitting room was opulent and even though it was twice the size of my living room, it seemed smaller because it was crammed with antique furnishings. It was also empty. I didn't know whether her bedroom was the one on the right or the one on the left.

"Pauline," I called.

"Leave me alone."

The voice came from the room to the left whose door was slightly ajar. I knocked on it perfunctorily and went in. Pauline was lying face down across the queen-sized bed. Setting the tray on the round table covered with a cloth that matched the flowered drapes, I poured the tea.

"This will make you feel better," I said, walking to the bed.

Pauline sat up, glowering at me. "I doubt that," she snapped. "The least you could have done was bring me a vodka tonic. Annette, that skinny witch, is watching me like a hawk, daring me to take a drink."

"Sorry, I didn't know that's what you wanted." Her husband's murderer had taken a gin and tonic. Casually I asked. "Do you ever drink gin and tonic?"

"Only if there's no vodka. Why?"

"Just wondered. Here's your tea. It's better for you than alcohol since you'll have to go back down to see your guests."

"Oh God," she muttered, burying her face in her hands. "Why don't they go home?"

"They will. In an hour it'll all be over. You can hang in there till then. You can do it. Here. Drink this."

She looked up at me, her strange, yellow-green eyes distrustful, yet I sensed she wanted to trust, to reach out to someone. Who in this house would show her any kindness? After a moment's hesitation, she took the cup from me, sloshing a little tea into the saucer. Ignoring that, she took a couple of sips. Shuddering, she said, "This stuff is as vile as medicine."

I had never thought of orange pekoe in those terms but to a non-tea drinker it might taste that way. Up close, I noticed that Pauline had aged in the past week. The strain probably accounted for the downward slant of her mouth, and the exhaustion in the set of her shoulders suggested sleepless nights. Perhaps she wasn't as unfeeling and tough as she pretended to be.

"What are your immediate plans?" I asked. Her answer was prompt.

"Get away from here. This house. This town. Go some place where the sun shines. A cruise, maybe. Yeah, a cruise through the Caribbean islands."

I tried to hide my shocked reaction. She was going on the cruise she'd planned to take with her husband. This struck me as completely insensitive if not downright macabre.

"Alone?" I asked.

"Of course, alone. What kind of question is that? Who did you think I'd go with?"

I saw my question had made her both angry and defensive.

"My husband just died, for Christ's sake."

I studied Pauline closely, observing the tremor of her hands that hadn't been there before.

"I have no family. Who could I take? Answer me that."

"I don't know, but you don't seem the type who would enjoy a cruise alone. I thought maybe you'd take a girlfriend."

She leaped on that suggestion. "That's a good idea. I might just do that."

Pauline was lying. She was taking someone on that cruise, and it wasn't a woman. Had she been carrying on a love affair all along? Had my hunch been right when Ariosto summoned me to the house on the day of his murder? Had he been ready to hire me to find out who his wife's lover was? I hadn't like the idea then and I didn't like it now, but that would provide Pauline with a motive to kill her husband. Or more likely, to have him killed. I didn't want to believe that even as the thought wormed its way through my brain.

"You may take this back down with you," she said, dismissing me as if I were the upstairs maid.

"I'll take it when I leave." There was one more subject I needed to discuss with her. "So, you're a lover of classical music," I said casually.

"What?"

"The Chicago Symphony." Watching her eyes, I knew the moment she realized where I was headed. It didn't seem to frighten her.

"Oh, yeah, the symphony. When Terrance couldn't go, Harry volunteered. He really knows a lot about classical music. Did you know he wanted to study music? But Terrance wouldn't let him. Said it was a waste of time because there's no money in it. I suppose he was right about that. Terrance was always right about money if nothing else." Her voice was bitter.

"Did you take the toll road to Chicago?" I asked.

"Yes. We parked in a garage on Randolph Street and walked to Orchestra Hall."

I wondered why she volunteered that. To strengthen an alibi for the night her husband was shot? "Did you drive?"

"No. Harry did. He made good time in that car of his."

"What does he drive?"

"A Ferrari." Pauline was silent, lost in thought. After a while she said, "I never imagined…"

"What?" I prompted.

She pulled herself together. "Nothing. Why are you asking me these questions?"

I shrugged. "Making conversation. You looked ill and upset. I thought you might want someone to talk to." I rose from the chair and picked up the tray.

"I'll go down with you, if you wait a minute." Pauline crossed to her dressing table which looked like a display counter in Marshall Field's cosmetic section. With somewhat unsteady hands she reapplied burgundy lipstick, dusted her cheeks with blush, fluffed up her silver streaked hair and announced she was ready to face the mob downstairs.

After I deposited the tray in the kitchen, I looked for Harry. When I couldn't find him, I drove to the agency, forming theories and discarding them as fast as I made them.

I reported to Uncle Barney. Since I had surveillance duty that night, I dashed home right after that and fixed a turkey sandwich and a thermos of strong coffee.

AT THE DOLPHIN I parked next to Glenn's car. He formed a zero with his thumb and index finger, signaling no activity had taken place in Room 18. Then he threw me a brisk two-finger salute and drove away.

Settling in as comfortably as I could, I picked up the sweater I was knitting for Luke for Christmas. Since I was working on the back which called for nothing more complicated than alternating rows of knit and purl, I could do this in the near-dark of the car. It helped pass my four hour stint and kept me from nodding off.

At midnight Uncle Barney took over. I drove home, went to bed, and read for an hour before I turned the light out.

Loud pounding woke me. Glancing at my clock, I saw that it was three minutes to seven. Who on earth was making that racket? I ran downstairs and flung the front door open.

"Luke?" I managed to say after I recovered from my surprise. "What are you doing?" I paused. "I mean I *see* that you're hammering on my porch railing, but why?"

He paused and straightened up. "Because your railing

is loose. One of these dark nights you might stumble, grab for it, and it'll collapse. You could get hurt."

"Oh. I know it's loose. My handyman promised to fix it. He must have forgotten."

"Don't tell me you hired Muttering Manny as your handyman?"

"Okay, so I won't tell you. And don't glower at me."

Luke shook his head. "Cybil, the man is unreliable. Half the time he doesn't know where he is. The other half he thinks he's waiting for orders to go to 'Nam."

"He's not that bad. If he were, the V.A. Hospital wouldn't have released him. And he needs the money."

"No, he doesn't. He only spends it on cheap liquor."

"I don't actually give him cash. Usually I feed him a meal as part of his payment and send the rest to Father Joseph who looks out for him."

Luke nodded approvingly. "But Manny is still unreliable. You need to hire someone who'll actually show up when he's supposed to."

"I have. Several times. I never realized how hard it was to hire good help...." My voice trailed off. That's exactly what Luke had told me years earlier when I had wanted to buy the old Victorian house one street over. From the gleam in his dark eyes I knew he remembered that. "Are you going to say 'I told you so'?"

"No, I'd never say that to you."

Luke grinned at me. He really has an adorable grin. I had almost forgotten that. He hammered a nail into place.

"I'm surprised you were still asleep. You're usually up with the sun," he said.

"And you sleep until the last possible minute. Why are you up so early?"

"I couldn't sleep."

I looked at him carefully. "How come? You're usually asleep thirty seconds after your head hits the pillow."

"I'm changing shifts. It always takes me a few days to adjust."

I didn't believe him. Or not entirely. I also knew from the set of his shoulders that he wouldn't elaborate. Luke isn't a stubborn man ordinarily, but once he's made up his mind, he usually doesn't budge. By the way he stood, I knew this was one of those times. Had I contributed to turning him into an insomniac?

"How about you? Why were you still in bed at seven in the morning?" he asked. "Couldn't you sleep? How long have you had this problem again? I don't want to give you pills, but I know of a clinic that deals with sleep disorders and has had good results with other methods."

"I just went to bed late. That's all. I don't need a clinic." Luke didn't look as if he believed me. "I had surveillance duty last night and didn't go to bed until nearly two."

"Surveillance? Alone? In the middle of the night?"

Luke whacked the nail with unnecessary force. The railing shuddered. Another whack like that one and I would need a whole new railing. "Luke, I was in no danger. Do you think Uncle Barney would send me some place where I could get hurt?" He gave me a long, hard look.

"No, I guess not."

"You want to come in for coffee?" I asked.

He glanced at his watch. "I'd love to, but I better get going." He picked up the bag of nails and turned to go.

"Luke?" He turned back. "Thanks for fixing the railing. And thanks for caring." He looked as if he wanted to say something but changed his mind. He waved and walked to his car. I watched him drive away.

UNCLE BARNEY AND THE OTHER agents who'd been on watch at The Dolphin had nothing to report when I went to the office.

I puttered around for a while, cleaned out my in-basket, straightened out some files in my drawer and filled out my expense account. When my desk looked as bare as Mother Hubbard's cupboard, I realized I couldn't stand not doing anything.

Even though I knew Sam had sent Sergeant Griffin to check Pauline's alibi, I would double check it. I had no other leads to follow, no clues that meant anything to me. Besides, I like Chicago. Spending a couple of hours there wouldn't be a hardship at all.

I took the toll road as far as Lake Station, swung off onto the Chicago Skyway to Stony Island and hit Lake Shore Drive after passing the Museum of Science and Industry. I know Sandburg called Chicago the "hog butcher of the world" but in the years that have passed since then, enormous changes have taken place. This city is now as exciting and elegant as any in the country. At least to me it is.

I parked in the same garage on Randolph Street

Pauline used. Unfortunately, the two men on duty Saturday night wouldn't report for work for another three hours. It was also too early to visit Orchestra Hall. Glancing at my watch, I knew I couldn't get back in time to cook dinner and be ready for the stakeout at eight. Thank heaven for take-out food and delis.

I retrieved my car and drove toward the Lincoln Park area and my favorite deli which specializes in central European imports, including Austria's Stiegl beer. I also stocked up on sausages, cheeses and the pungent black bread Maxi and Uncle Barney like. Anticipating their pleasure, I smiled.

When I returned to the parking garage, the two attendants, their hair cropped close with initials shaved into it, had arrived. Both in their early twenties, they exaggerated their cool walk until it was a parody of itself. I identified myself and told them why I needed the information.

"Do you remember parking an unusual car with Indiana license plates last Saturday night?"

They exchanged a significant look.

"What's the matter?" I asked.

"Somebody else asked about that," the shorter of the two said. The initials on his head read "ALM".

"A cop? Tall, thin, sneezes a lot?"

Both nodded. I took out two ten-dollar bills and held them up. "What about the car?"

"Italian wheels. Real cool," ALM said.

"Most expensive sports job I've seen around here," initials DRG added.

"Blood-red with jet black leather interior."

"Do you remember the make?" I asked.

"Uh-huh. Sonny Crockett wheels."

"Pardon?" I saw them exchange a look that clearly conveyed their opinion of my ignorance.

"Sonny Crockett on 'Miami Vice' drives a car like that."

"A Ferrari," ALM added with exaggerated patience.

"Oh." "Miami Vice" had to be on reruns somewhere. "This Ferrari. Did it stay in this garage all evening?" I asked.

"Sure did. The young dude driving it gave us twenty bucks each to keep an eye on it."

"What did he look like?"

ALM shrugged. "All whities look alike."

They laughed uproariously at this witty observation. I waited until they recovered.

"Was someone with him? A woman perhaps?"

"The dude was alone."

"When did he drop the car off?"

"About ten to eight," DRG said.

"When did he pick it up?"

"Around eleven-thirty."

According to Sergeant Griffin's report, Pauline and Harry had stopped for a sandwich and a drink after the concert. That accounted easily for the time that elapsed between the concert and the time they retrieved the car.

"Thanks." I handed each a bill and walked south to Orchestra Hall. I told the woman in the office what I needed. Obligingly she looked up the usher who worked that section of seats.

"That's Thelma Young's area, but this is her day off."

"I've got to speak to her. It's really important." I

exaggerated a little, saying that an innocent woman might go to jail if I couldn't talk to Thelma. "I know you can't give out addresses of your employees, but could you call her? I'll pay for her time if she'll see me."

"Well, I guess I could do that."

Five minutes later I was on my way to the garage. My two attendants had taken good care of the Volvo for which I tipped them generously.

Thelma lived in Rogers Park. After consulting the map of the city, I drove north on Lake Shore Drive, then swung west. Apparently Thelma had been watching from the window. She opened the door before I had a chance to knock.

"Come in," she said, tying the belt on a green satin robe. "I just got up. Don't mind the mess."

Her efficiency apartment seemed anything but efficient, probably because of the mess she'd referred to. I wondered if she ever hung up any of her clothes or just tossed them into piles of dirty, so-so, and clean. She lit a cigarette.

"Want some coffee?" Thelma asked. "It's only instant."

"No, thank you," I said hastily. I watched her dump a half teaspoon of instant coffee powder into the mug, add water from a kettle that couldn't be anywhere near boiling and sip the weak-looking brew. Maxi would be horrified at what Thelma called coffee.

"So, you want to pay me for information," she said, looking at me over the rim of the mug.

"No, I want to pay you for your time while I ask you questions, the answers to which I expect to be truthful."

Thelma shrugged. "Have it your way. I have no reason to lie. How much are you paying? Not that I wouldn't cooperate without it, but a girl can always use the extra cash. I'm going to school part time. Another year and I'll be a dental hygienist."

"Will twenty dollars for five minutes of your time cover it?"

"Could you make it twenty-five?"

"Sure," I agreed and pulled the bills from my wallet.

"What do you want to know about Saturday?" she asked.

"Whether two people attended the symphony that night. The family's had the same seats for years. In your section, twelfth row, seats five and six. The same people don't necessarily attend each time."

"Last Saturday," she said, closing her eyes in concentration. "Yeah. The woman arrived first. She had this gorgeous silver cape slung across one shoulder." Thelma sashayed across the room, her hips swaying in imitation of the woman's sensuous glide. "He didn't get there until the last minute. Slipped me a five, so I showed him to his seat even though I should have made him wait in the foyer." She paused a moment. Then she giggled. "The movie star. Or gigolo."

"Pardon?"

"It's a game I play. Trying to guess what people do. He was so good-looking he could have been a movie star."

"What about the gigolo?"

"He could have been that, too. The woman he was

with wore enough jewelry to be able to afford him. She was also older than him. Not much, but a few years."

"Did they stay for the entire concert?"

"That I don't know. All I know for sure is that they were there at the beginning. That I can swear to in a court of law."

It didn't really matter if they stayed for all of the performance or not. They couldn't have driven back to Westport, shot Ariosto and returned in time to get the car out of the garage at eleven-thirty. Besides, the Ferrari had remained in the garage. Even if Pauline had driven a second car to Chicago and they had used it, there still wasn't enough time.

"Well, thanks a lot." I handed Thelma her twenty-five dollars which she folded carefully and placed into the pocket of her robe.

So much for long shots. And double checking. And filling in time with action.

I MADE IT HOME IN JUST a little under three hours and in time to take the deli items to Maxi's farm. She insisted on grilling a couple of the sausages for us. I didn't try to talk her out of it. She added some of her cabbage cooked with white wine and dark bread for a simple but tasty meal. Armed with a thermos of her delicious coffee, I drove to The Dolphin.

This being Friday night, the motel filled up rapidly, but Room 18 remained unoccupied.

It was a perfect Bulwer-Lytton night: the wind howled and intermittent rain squalls hurled sheets of water against the windshield, rendering the dark night even more impenetrable. I turned on my tiny reading light, certain that its meager beam couldn't be seen outside the car. With it on the seat next to me, I could knit. During one of these downpours, a car slid into the parking slot before Room 18. Dropping my knitting on the passenger seat, I slipped out of the Volvo. Carefully I closed the door with a soft click. I skirted the parked cars and dashed to the relative protection of the stairs leading to the rooms. From there I could see the room without getting blinded by the rain.

The figure emerging from the light-colored Mercedes struggled briefly with a wind-tossed umbrella before hurling it back into the car. Mentally I reviewed the list I'd made of all vehicles belonging to the Ariosto family. It included an off-white Mercedes. I watched the dark shape run to the door. From the small waist, accentuated by the tightly belted raincoat, I was certain the Mercedes' driver was a woman. My guess was confirmed when she pushed back the hood to unlock the door. Just before entering, she looked around nervously and I recognized her: Pauline Ariosto.

Even though part of me half expected her, I was still dismayed. I didn't want it to be Pauline. When I realized what I was doing, I chided myself. My job wasn't to approve or disapprove of people and their activities. I'd been hired to clear Annette. Nothing more.

Grimly I stepped farther into the recess behind the stairs to wait. I took the camera from my pocket and slipped the strap around my neck. Chances were I wouldn't recognize Pauline's lover. A photo would help us identify him. If the light spilling from the open door was strong enough for a photograph.

Burying my hands deep in the pockets of my raincoat,

I shivered. It seemed to turn chillier by the minute with the kind of wet cold that penetrates all layers of clothing. Whoever Pauline's lover was, I hoped he was the impatient type.

He wasn't. Twenty-six minutes elapsed before I heard footsteps. Pressing myself as far into the dark corner as I could, I hoped my chattering teeth wouldn't betray my presence.

From the way he moved, he was young and in a hurry. As soon as his rapid strides moved past the stairs, I stepped forward to watch him approach Room 18. From the back I couldn't tell much about him, but his lean, jean-and-black-leather jacket-clad body reinforced my opinion of his youthfulness. Stealthily I followed him a few steps.

Pauline must have been waiting by the door for as soon as he knocked, she flung it wide open and threw herself into his arms. When she pulled back to look at him, the light from the room fell full on his face. I gasped, feeling as if someone had knocked the air out of my lungs.

TWELVE

HARRY ARIOSTO.

Stepmother and stepson. Lovers.

I couldn't believe it, not even after I saw them exchange a passionate kiss before Pauline pulled Harry into the room. I kept staring at the spot where they had stood long after the door closed behind them.

Eventually I roused myself to action. I had to call Uncle Barney. There was no sense now in him driving all the way to the motel to relieve me. I dashed back to my car and phoned him. He wasn't in, so I left a message on his machine, asking him to wait for me at my house.

I got the car's heater going full blast. Water squeaked in my loafers. My jeans flapped soggily against my calves. Few things are more uncomfortable than cold, wet denim, I reflected, trying to wring water from the stiff material.

After the car was toasty, I switched the motor off. There was no real reason for me to stay, yet I was reluctant to leave. The temperature dropped quickly inside the car, forcing me to run the motor at fifteen-minute intervals.

At ten-thirty the lovers emerged. Harry waited solicitously until Pauline drove off before he turned up his collar and darted toward the far parking lot. Something compelled me to follow him with my headlights off. Fully expecting to see the Sonny Crockett car, I was surprised when Harry unlocked a blue 1986 Mustang. I entered the license plate number in my notebook. I didn't know quite how, but Harry having access to a second car might be important in solving the case. If we ever solved it.

Before I left the motel, I had to find out in whose name Room 18 was rented and what the arrangement was. Pauline had arrived, key in hand. I had the other key, left to me by Sidney who, I suspected, pilfered it from one of the lovers.

A glimmer of an idea came to me but it involved use of a phone book. I drove toward Michigan City. At a well-lit convenience store I spied an inside pay phone. Luck was with me. A telephone directory with all pages intact was chained to the wall. After I located what I needed in the florists' section of the yellow pages, I dialed the motel's number.

"Hello. This is Blossoms Unlimited. We have a delivery for the party in Room 18 but I can't read the name. My assistant's writing looks like chicken scratches. Honestly, it's impossible to get good help anymore," I complained.

"I know what you mean. It's the same in the motel business. Did you say Room 18?"

"Yes, sir." I pressed the receiver against my ear, praying the man on the other end wouldn't change his mind. He didn't.

"Let's see," he said. "Room 18 is reserved for Paul Greco."

"Thank you so much. This is very kind of you."

Paul Greco was certainly a more imaginative alias than the usual Brown, Smith or Jones. Driving toward Westport, I kept wondering how he'd hit upon that name.

At home, Uncle Barney's car was parked in front of my house. He joined me. I lit the fire I had laid earlier. The heat from the fire warmed my outstretched hands. Despite its warmth, I shivered.

"What's wrong, Cybil?"

Even though I had my back turned to Uncle Barney, he could tell that I was tense. I turned to face him. "Room 18 had visitors tonight. A pair of lovers."

"I'm not surprised," he said wearily. "Who?"

"Pauline Ariosto. Subconsciously at least, I expected her to show up."

"Why didn't you tell me?" Barney demanded.

"It was only a hunch. Maybe only half a hunch, if that's possible."

"It is. Never discount hunches, Cybil. Not even partial ones." Barney took his pipe from his tweed jacket and fiddled with it. "Who joined her?" he asked, his curiosity carefully restrained.

"Now that's the kicker. I never even considered this man for the role of her lover." Though I knew he was waiting for my answer, I had to take a couple of deep breaths.

"Who, Cybil?" Barney asked again, but his voice was gentle.

"Harry Ariosto."

"Jesus H. Christ!"

Uncle Barney is the cleanest-mouthed man I know.

This exclamation came as close to swearing as I've ever heard him come.

"Pauline's stepson?"

"Yes. It's like that Greek story of Phaedra. Do you remember it?"

"No."

"As I recall, Phaedra fell in love with her stepson." I shook my head, bemused. "I wonder how long ago that's supposed to have happened." I walked to the adjoining library whose only furniture consisted of the glass-fronted, built-in bookshelves. I reached for a dictionary of mythology. "It says here that the accepted date for the Trojan War is around 1290 B.C. The Phaedra story occurs in the generation preceding the war. How many years ago is that?"

"Around three thousand," Barney said.

"Imagine. All those centuries between then and now and still we see the same triangle situation, the same passions." I shook my head.

"I've found that human nature is pretty much the same the world over. I guess it's timeless as well." Barney tapped the bitten end of his cold pipe against his jaw. "I don't suppose you could be mistaken about the nature of their relationship?"

"No. The kiss I witnessed was anything but familial. Besides, why would they need a motel room if they weren't lovers? I wish I were mistaken," I heard myself add somewhat wistfully.

"Why?" Barney wanted to know.

I hadn't thought about that before. I shrugged. "I don't know, except I like Harry. And it's not only because he looks like a Greek god."

"A Greek god?" Barney's left eyebrow rose.

"We were speaking about Greek mythology," I said quickly.

"Well, that certainly gives both of them a strong motive for murder," Barney said.

"Yes, but no opportunity. There's no way they could have come back to Westport, shot Ariosto, and returned to Chicago. It's not possible."

"Don't be so sure," Barney warned. "Just because we haven't been able to figure out how it was done, doesn't mean it can't be done. Do we have anybody else whose motive is anywhere near as powerful?"

"No. For a short while Dunn and Fettner looked like good candidates but both have alibis. I'm sure neither Annette nor Ramsey did it, even though Ramsey has no alibi and Annette is unwilling to name hers."

"Get her to disclose it to you. We have to clear Annette completely. Recheck Ramsey Ariosto also. Somebody must have seen him or spoken to him that evening. Then we'll take the Chicago trip apart. In my experience, criminals always make a small mistake. The trick is to find it."

"All right."

"What do you know about Harry?" Barney asked.

"Very little. He's a senior at the university. Drives a Ferrari. Didn't stand up to Terrance Ariosto according to Annette. I saw Harry and his stepfather together once. Ariosto treated him shabbily but then he treated most people that way. Mrs. Dougherty likes Harry. She said he did well in school until the spring semester when he…" I paused, knowing now with whom he fell in love. "When he fell in love."

"So, we know approximately when the affair started. Since it's lasted this long, it's apparently more than a little fling," Barney said, his voice thoughtful.

The words "little fling" didn't strike me as being appropriate, not when the fling seemed to be connected to the deaths of three men. With that horrendous toll, nothing less than the term grand passion would do.

"Cybil, didn't you used to know someone on campus?"

"I still do."

"See what you can find out about Harry. Discreetly, of course. We don't want to spook anyone into doing something foolish."

"I can't see either Pauline or Harry using a shotgun to kill three people. At least not personally."

"You think they hired someone?"

"Yes."

Barney clamped his teeth around the stem of his pipe the way he does when he concentrates. After a while he said, "I don't think so. It's not as easy to hire a hitman as television programs suggest. I doubt that either Pauline or Harry have the kind of connections it takes to find an assassin."

"What about those awful macho survival magazines? Some of their ads are very suggestive," I pointed out.

"True. Still, I don't think these murders were committed by professionals. The weapon's all wrong, for one thing."

"For another?" I queried.

"At least two of the victims probably opened their doors to the murderer. None of the three put up a fight which suggests that they knew the killer and didn't anticipate danger." Barney glanced at his watch. "It's getting late. Tomorrow we'll concentrate on this case exclusively. If you need help with the legwork, let me know."

I walked Uncle Barney to the front door.

THE NEXT MORNING I drove to the YWCA and forced myself to swim thirty laps. I needed the physical exertion to balance the emotional stress of the case.

After that I drove to Ramsey's apartment. I had left a message on his machine the night before, so he knew I was coming.

Ramsey opened the door promptly, freshly shaved and showered judging by the smell of soap and aftershave that wafted from him. He wore jeans with paint stains that seemed to have withstood repeated laundering and a red-and-white Indiana University sweatshirt.

"I'm making coffee. Do you mind talking in the kitchen?"

"Not at all."

He offered me orange juice which I declined. Ramsey sipped his while setting out mugs, spoons, milk and sugar on the small butcher block table in the breakfast nook. As soon as the coffee maker stopped dripping, he brought the pot to the table along with a box of chocolate chip cookies. He held the opened box toward me. I shook my head, suppressing the shudder his idea of breakfast evoked.

"What can I do for you?" Ramsey popped a whole cookie into his mouth.

"We would like to eliminate you from our list of suspects. Let me finish, please," I said when he stopped chewing and looked at me wide-eyed. "I don't think you shot your uncle but my believing that isn't good enough. We need proof. We have to verify your alibi. I want you to concentrate on last Saturday. Tell me everything you did from the minute you woke up to the moment you fell asleep."

Ramsey munched a couple of cookies before he spoke. "I slept late that morning because I'd been to a party the night before. When I got up and looked in my fridge for something to eat, all I found was beer, a small tub of margarine and a bottle of ketchup. I decided it was time to go to the grocery store. On my way back, I stopped at the International House of Pancakes for brunch. After I put the groceries away I did a couple of loads of laundry."

He paused in his recitation to eat another cookie and think. I sipped my coffee.

"I don't remember in what order I did these things, but I wrote checks to cover some bills, took out the garbage and bundled up a bunch of newspapers for re-cycling. Later I watched the Notre Dame-U.S.C. football game. After that I popped a frozen pizza in the oven and worked on my report. I had reservations at the country club for dinner, but as I told you, my date got sick. So I stayed home. That is, until the police called me, wanting to know where the rest of the family was. I told them about Pauline and Harry being in Chicago and the staff having the evening off."

"Think back to the early part of the evening. Did anyone phone you? Come to the door to sell you something?" I could tell by the surprised look on his face that Ramsey had remembered something.

"How could I have been so dumb?" Ramsey looked at the cookie box, stunned. Then a wide, happy smile settled on his face. "Cybil, I have an alibi! During the crucial half hour I bought cookies from a girl and allowed her to use my phone."

"Back up, Ramsey. Start at the beginning. What girl? How old?" It wouldn't help much if she was very young, I thought.

"She said her name was Nancy and she was selling cookies for their church. The profits would be used to pay for the youth group's travel expenses to a summer camp for underprivileged children where they would work as junior counselors. With a story like that how could I buy less than six boxes?"

"Right." I grinned back at him. "Tell me more about the girl."

"I didn't look at her that closely. She looked like all twelve or thirteen year olds look, I guess. You know, braces on her teeth. Wearing blue jeans and a parka."

"I bet if she'd been twenty-two instead of twelve you could describe her in great detail," I muttered. "What about the phone call?"

"I was her last customer. I got the impression that she'd stayed out longer than she'd planned and it had gotten dark. She asked if she could use the phone to call her mother to come and pick her up. Naturally, I said it was okay. Her mother wasn't home when she called the first time. I could tell she was afraid to go outside so I asked her to wait in my living room which she did. When she called home again a few minutes later, her mother was there and came right away."

"What time did she arrive?"

Ramsey smiled again. "Seven forty-five. I remember

I looked at my watch when she knocked on the door. Seven forty-five, Cybil. There's no way on earth I could have driven to my uncle's house and shot him."

"No, you couldn't. What is Nancy's last name?"

Ramsey's smile shrunk a little. "I don't know."

"What was the name of her church?"

This question killed his smile. "I don't remember."

"Think, Ramsey."

He shook his head, looking unhappy. "United something. Maybe."

"Don't give up. We'll figure it out yet. From what you said, Nancy was walking from apartment to apartment?"

"Yes."

"How long did it take her mother to get to your place?"

"Ten minutes at the most."

"And she came up to your apartment?"

"Yes."

"Mmm. Let's see. She got Nancy's call, grabbed her purse and car keys, drove over, parked and walked up here. If she did all this in ten minutes, she can't live very far away."

"True, but how does that help?"

"At the agency we'll call every church in town till we find the one whose youth group is selling these cookies. I'm sure there won't be more than one Nancy in that age bracket. We'll get in touch with her and have her verify your alibi. Simple, isn't it?"

AND IT WAS. With four of us telephoning, it took only thirty minutes to locate the church using cookies as a fundraiser. Fortunately, Barney knew the pastor whom he persuaded to disclose Nancy's last name and address.

The Taylors lived on the near northeast side which meant I was there in less than fifteen minutes. The pastor had phoned Mrs. Taylor. She shooed the two girls watching television out of the living room and invited me to sit in the best armchair. Perching on the edge of the matching couch, she looked at me anxiously.

"I won't take much of your time," I said with a re-assuring smile. "I only need to verify something. Did you pick up Nancy at Ramsey Ariosto's apartment two Saturday nights ago at seven forty-five?"

Mrs. Taylor nodded, her face growing more anxious. "I've told that girl time and again to get herself home before dark. Anything could happen to her out on the streets. This town isn't as safe as it used to be when I was Nancy's age." She shook her head and sighed before she continued. "But she's bound and determined to sell the most cookies and win the contest. When she called from that nice Mr. Ariosto's apartment, I rushed right over to pick her up."

"Did you look at your watch to check the time?"

"Well, no. I'm allergic to every kind of watchband I ever tried, so I gave up wearing watches. But Mr. Ar-ioso's clock on the wall chimed the time when we were there. I remember thinking that I'd have to get the lead out if I wanted to finish decorating the cupcakes for Sunday school."

I'd seen the antique clock in Ramsey's living room. "Well, thank you so much, Mrs. Taylor. I won't hold up your lunch any longer."

I had cleared Ramsey Ariosto. One down and one to go. Glancing at my watch, I decided to grab a bite to eat before I tackled Annette and got her to admit she hadn't spent the night of her father's murder alone.

The Horn of Plenty, Westport's only natural foods cum vegetarian restaurant, is always crowded which is the only thing I hold against it. This being Saturday with the downtown area relatively deserted, I had to wait only ten minutes for a table. I used the time to phone Uncle Barney and report on my interview with Mrs. Taylor. After enjoying the Horn's marinated vegetable plate and multigrain muffins, I drove to the Ariosto estate.

Once again Annette asked me to join her for a walk even though it was a cold, overcast late October day.

"I know why you're here," she said.

"Oh?"

"Ramsey called. He talked to your uncle who confirmed that his alibi has been established. I figured you're here to verify mine."

"Yes." I saw Annette shiver and zip up her coat.

"I don't want anyone to hear what I have to tell you."

"I understand."

"I don't know how to say this exactly."

"Straight out is usually the best," I encouraged.

Looking at me, she asked, "Are you still married to that good-looking doctor?"

"Yes, but we're separated." I didn't know what my marriage to Luke had to do with anything.

"Maybe then you'll understand. Or maybe you'll condemn me." Annette laughed, but it was a joyless laughter.

"I've been married for eight years. My husband's a good man, but…" She shrugged. "Anyway, I never planned to cheat on him. It just happened. I met this man and before I knew what happened, we were involved. It was so heady, so exciting to feel young and desirable again. At least, it was then. But if I get through this with my marriage in one piece, I'll break off the affair as soon as I get back to Detroit."

"You spent that Saturday night with this man, didn't you?"

"Yes."

We continued to walk in silence, rounding the tennis court.

"Do you have to know his name, Cybil?"

"Not now. Maybe not even later. I'll let you know." Annette didn't display her emotions often but this time she was visibly relieved. "How long do you plan to stay in Westport?"

"Until this is cleared up. The police politely but firmly advised me not to leave town. My husband and children are flying back tonight."

"Let's hope you can join them soon. I have to speak to Pauline. Is she here?"

"No. She went to the Sports Club a while ago."

We walked toward the back door.

"I came across an odd thing," Annette said. "I was paying the household bills, including charges to various charge accounts. My father's gold card listed the purchase of a shotgun. The kind used to kill him."

I stopped walking. "That is strange. What was the date of the charge?"

"The Monday before my father was killed."

The day after Crawford was shot. "Is the shotgun in the house?"

"Yes."

"Did you report this to the police?"

"Yes. They had already examined all the guns in the house."

Strange indeed. Why would anyone buy a gun identical to the one used to kill the head accountant? No reason unless…yes, that made sense. To replace the murder weapon taken from the gunrack. That meant that someone from the house had shot Crawford which brought me back to Pauline and Harry.

At the backdoor I said goodbye to Annette.

THE SPORTS CLUB IS an exclusive organization dedicated to the pursuit of the more esoteric sports. That's all I knew about it. That and its approximate location out in the fields northeast of the city. I found the club with only a few wrong turns.

Driving slowly around its perimeter, I saw that it was enclosed by a tall fence warning against trespassing. I suspected that the fence was electrified. At the entrance gate an armed, uniformed guard stood watch. He didn't look friendly, I thought, as I drove past.

I parked on the nearest side road. Across from the entrance the large corn field was bare but the bushes lining the ditch bordering the road offered enough protection to hide my approach. At least I hoped they did as I ran in a low crouch to a spot across from the gate. Keeping low, I watched.

The guard checked the identification of the driver and any passengers before raising the ramp to admit the vehicle. Why such tight security? Probably to protect the privacy of the members who no doubt paid a big enough fee for it. But why use an armed guard? His presence intrigued me enough to make me determined to take a closer look at the club.

The arrival of a laundry truck gave me the idea of how to get in. I had to wait an hour before the right vehicle pulled up to the gate. The pickup truck delivering salt for the club's water softeners was ideal. At it slowed down, I sprinted across the road. I caught up with it as it came to a full stop. Swinging myself over the tailgate, I fell on a bag of salt. I held my breath, fearing the guard might have heard the thump with which I'd landed.

"You're late today."

The guard's voice.

"Yeah. This is my last stop."

This accounted for the few sacks on the truck. Lucky for me. If the truck had been fully loaded, I couldn't have hidden in it. I only hoped the guard wouldn't decide to spot check. I flattened against the sack as much as possible, hardly breathing until the driver put the truck in gear. When I was sure the truck was out of sight of the guard, I risked a look.

We were approaching the back of a building, obviously the truck's destination. As soon as it slowed down, I climbed over the tailgate and dropped to the ground. Even though I landed hard, I managed to roll and sprint to the cover offered by a parked van. When no one raised the alarm, I brushed off my slacks and headed for the center of the complex as though I had every right to be there.

THIRTEEN

TWO MEN PASSED ME, shotguns resting easily on their shoulders. Intrigued, I followed them at a discreet distance. We passed a sign pointing north, labeled skeet shooting. Just about at the same time I heard shots at equally timed intervals. We walked through a wooded area for about two hundred yards, I estimated, before we reached the target range.

I had no trouble spotting Pauline. She wore a yellow down vest over an olive-green jumpsuit. With the gun at her shoulder, I heard her yell "pull". A fraction of a second later the saucer-shaped clay target splintered in the air. In the time I watched her, which must have been a good five minutes, Pauline didn't miss a single target. The woman was a deadly accurate shot.

Apparently the round or whatever it was called, was over for Pauline lowered the gun. I took advantage of the lull to speak to her.

"You do this very well," I commented.

Pauline jumped, startled by my voice. She wheeled around. From the scowl on her face I deduced that she wasn't glad to see me, but she forced herself to be civil. She even managed a brittle smile when she greeted me.

"Have you been shooting long?" I asked.

"Terrance introduced me to the sport. Seems like it comes naturally to me."

"Do you enter competitions?"

"Sure. I've won quite a few trophies over the years."

She said this with obvious pride. Pauline looked better than she had the last time I saw her. The cold, fresh air had put color into her cheeks and her hair glittered silvery. She must have had it freshly streaked, I decided.

"How did you find me?"

"Annette told me where you were."

"Well, I'm busy. What do you want?" Pauline turned away, preparing to shoot again.

"Why did you buy a shotgun to replace the one missing from the gun cabinet in the game room?"

Pauline whirled around, the gun pointing at my head. For a terrifying moment I wondered if she was going to shoot. Involuntarily, my body arched away from her. After a tense moment, Pauline slowly lowered the gun.

"I don't know what you're talking about. What makes you think I bought a gun?" she demanded, her eyes and voice flat.

"Because you made the mistake of charging it. My guess is that you phoned the order in and the company demanded a credit card number. That shows how desperate you were to get a look-alike gun into the rack. Why? What happened to the original? The one used to kill Galen Crawford? It was never reported stolen."

Pauline paled a little but otherwise retained remarkable control. This was one cool woman, I thought with a trace of admiration. Not that I had expected her to fall apart and confess on the spot.

"I repeat. I don't know what you're talking about."

Knowing I wasn't going to get a thing out of her, I acknowledged temporary defeat with a small nod in her direction. Then I turned and walked away. At the edge of the wood I paused. I heard Pauline call "pull". This time the clay target fell to earth unscathed. Out of the next ten shots she missed six. My questions had rattled her more than a little.

On my way back to the center of the club, I spotted a familiar figure, one I had left only hours earlier. Ramsey, bow in hand and quiver slung from a belt, disappeared around the corner of a building. Was the entire Ariosto family members of this club? Before I consciously realized what I was doing, I was in full pursuit of Ramsey.

Staying well back from the archery range, I watched him. In a flowing, continuous movement he fitted an arrow, raised the bow, aimed, anchored his right hand against his cheek and released the arrow smoothly. It pierced the target with a sharp thunk. I looked on, fascinated, as he repeated the process with a deliberate rhythm and astonishing accuracy that suggested a shooting machine. After a short time the bull's eye looked like a porcupine's back. Could the accuracy with a bow and arrow be transferred to a shotgun? The question made me uneasy.

Adding to my unease was the problem of getting out of the club unseen. The salt delivery pickup was long gone, but the laundry truck, back doors wide open, was still parked near the spot where I'd jumped out of the pickup. I looked around casually before I leaped into the van. Crouching behind a canvas laundry hamper I waited. Five minutes later two bags were tossed in, the doors closed and the motor revved up. I stayed hidden until we passed through the guard ramp.

Unless I wanted to ride all the way into Westport, which would leave me with the problem of retrieving my car, I had to get out of the truck soon. Unfortunately, the driver was going too fast for me to jump out. I would have to wait until he reached the four-way stop at Spruce Lane. As soon as he slowed, I opened the door a little. Only the fact that I had braced myself in anticipation saved me from being flung out onto the asphalt. The moment he stopped, I jumped out and started hiking back to my car.

It was a good three mile walk and despite my brisk pace, I reached the Volvo thoroughly chilled. All I wanted was a long hot bath and a pot of steaming Darjeeling tea.

SUNDAY I MET TERESA LISTER for lunch in the faculty dining room on campus. We'd been roommates during our freshman year and probably would have lived together all four years except that I participated in the sophomore-year-of-study abroad which threw us out of sync. Absorbed in the Sunday *Inquirer,* Teresa didn't notice my approach until I sat next to her in the reception area of the dining room. We greeted each other affectionately before proceeding into the high-ceilinged, oak-paneled, vaguely medieval-looking dining room.

Over fruit salads topped with delicious frozen raspberry yogurt, we caught up with each other's lives.

Teresa told me that she'd been promoted. She'd leave Beaumont Hall for the dean of students' office and part-time lecturing on women's studies at the end of the fall semester. I congratulated her.

"So, what can I do for you?" Teresa asked the moment she had emptied her plate.

I grinned at her. "Some things never change. You're still as direct as ever, and you still inhale your food in record time," I said, glancing at my half-full plate.

She shrugged. "I don't see the point in changing either habit. Both save time."

"And you're still preoccupied with time. Don't you ever just vegetate?"

Teresa shook her head, setting her short, black curls into motion. Once again I observed that she was better looking now than she had been at eighteen. She had grown into the harshly attractive lines and planes of her face which had struck a discordant note in her youth. I could envision her as a stunning looking silver-haired, black-eyed septuagenarian when the rest of us looked merely faded and worn.

"Are you still sleuthing, Cybil?" Teresa asked.

"Yes."

"Good for you. I bet that's why you asked me to lunch even though there's no lecture or concert on campus, isn't it?"

I started to protest but had to admit that her shrewd observation was correct. We only met when there was also another reason for me to come to the university.

"It's okay, Cybil. I understand. I don't meet you in town either."

"That could change now that you live off campus,"

I hinted. Spooning up the last of the yogurt, I wished there were more. "Anyway, I do want some information from you. It's connected with a case I'm working on."

"What do you want to know?"

"Information on a student."

Teresa's straight, black eyebrows curved.

"It's nothing confidential," I assured her. "I know what sort of grades he's made. I want to know something about him as a person."

"What's his name?"

"Harry Ariosto."

"Ah. You're investigating the murder of his step-father."

"Yes. Do you know Harry?"

"As a matter of fact, I do. We make it a policy to talk with all students who've lost a family member."

"What did you think of Harry?"

Teresa was quiet for what seemed to me a long time. I finished my salad while waiting for her to speak.

"Have you met Harry?" Teresa asked.

"Yes."

"Then you know how handsome he is. The secretaries look sort of shell shocked every time he comes to the office."

"You've seen him several times? Why?"

"Because he's a troubled young man."

"I noticed the change in him, too," I murmured.

"What do you think caused the change?"

Guilt over committing adultery with his stepfather's wife, I thought. Aloud I said, "Guilt. Terrance Ariosto treated Harry abominably. I would guess the young man had some nasty thoughts about his stepfather while he was alive and now feels badly."

"I worked with Ariosto on several fundraisers," Teresa said and grimaced. "I've never met a more odious, obnoxious man. I confess I had a few unpleasant thoughts about him myself. You want to go to my office with me? I'll look at the notes I made during my meetings with Harry."

Naturally I agreed. Teresa insisted on driving. Since visitor's parking spaces around the administration building are usually filled even on Sunday, I didn't object. However, when she headed west, I was puzzled. "Isn't the Ad Building north of here?"

"It's faster this way. We miss two traffic lights."

I suppressed a smile.

In Teresa's office books not only filled the shelves, they were stacked on every conceivable surface. I moved a stack off her straight-backed visitor's chair and sat down. Index cards stuck between the pages marked the passages Teresa was researching.

"What are you working on?" I asked.

"The role of feminism in Latin America."

Teresa took a manila folder from the filing cabinet and studied it before she spoke. "I noted here that Harry appeared to be almost distraught the first time I spoke with him. During his subsequent visit he had himself more under control, but I had the impression that deep down he was still anxious and upset."

"What did he say about his stepfather?"

"That struck me as odd at the time. Harry's answers were… I don't know how to put it except to say that they were carefully formulated. You know, as though he had thought out each answer beforehand. The most spontaneous remark he made was about working for his stepfather during the summer."

"Oh? Where did he work and in what capacity?"

"Let me see." Teresa scanned the page. "At Tri State. Seems he was some sort of overseer at a warehouse."

Harry was the connection to Crawford. He had to be.

"In what residence hall does Harry live?"

"Alpha."

I must have looked stunned because Teresa asked if something was wrong. I shook my head. Harry had been in on the pilfering. He had to have been for Crawford himself to deliver the steaks to Alpha the evening I had tailed him.

"Well, that's about all I know about Harry that I'm at liberty to disclose," Teresa said, shutting the folder.

"Does Harry have a roommate?"

"Yes." Teresa glanced at the folder again. "Joe Martinello. Room 141, Alpha Hall. Their phone number is 5682."

"What? What was that number?" When Teresa looked a little surprised at my insistent tone, I apologized. "I'm sorry. I didn't mean to yell. Did you say 5682?"

"Why, yes."

How could I have been so dense? The prefix for all campus phones is 242. Everybody in Westport knows that. Everybody in northern Indiana knows that and that's why only the last four digits for a university phone are usually given. When I thought of all the time our agency spent trying to figure out what the number could be, I felt like laughing and crying at the same time. I thanked Teresa for her help but declined her offer to drive me back to my car. I had to think. Walking helps me sort out my thoughts.

It all had to have started this past summer when Harry worked at Tri State. Had he uncovered the pilfering and demanded a cut? Had he organized it? He could have, but I didn't think so. It didn't quite seem in character. More likely Crawford had tumbled across the illicit love affair and had blackmailed Harry into looking the other way while he organized the theft ring. Of course, Crawford had undoubtedly blackmailed Pauline and Harry into forking over silence money as well. According to the piece of paper I found behind the photo, the sums were considerable.

What had happened then? Had Crawford's demands escalated into the realm of the impossible? Uncle Barney said blackmailers often become so greedy that they back their victims into a corner where they have no choice but to turn against their exploiters. While all that made sense, I couldn't picture Harry shooting Crawford.

Maybe Harry's handsomeness blinded me to some character flaws. I didn't think so, but it wouldn't hurt to meet him and look at him with hard, unflinching eyes.

Ten minutes later I parked my car near Alpha Hall.

From the lobby I phoned Harry's room. He was out, but his roommate agreed to come down to talk to me. Joe Martinello, handsome in a dark-eyed, black-haired, Mediterranean way, was as unsuspicious and friendly as Harry probably had been before he got involved in adultery and murder.

"Have you noticed any changes in Harry?" I asked

Joe after we'd arranged ourselves in the uncomfort-able, modern chairs grouped around a low glass-topped table.

"Yeah. He's as tightly wired as a coil. I keep telling him to lighten up, but he can't. I'm getting worried about him."

The concern Joe felt for Harry was clearly mirrored in his eyes. "How long have you known him?"

"We started rooming together at the beginning of our junior year, but I met him the year before."

"When did you notice Harry getting uptight?"

Joe answered without hesitation. "When I arrived on campus at the end of August."

"Has his anxiety increased since then, or remained the same?"

"It's gotten worse. Especially lately. With his father being killed and all…" Joe broke off, shaking his head.

Since he was obviously glad to have a chance to talk about his concern for Harry, I continued to probe. "Did his anxiety increase even before his father's death?"

Joe wrinkled his forehead in concentration. "Yeah, it did. I'd been attributing it all to his father's murder, but you're right. He got more nervous and worried even before his dad died."

"About a week earlier?"

Joe stared at me, eyes widened in surprise. "How did you know that?"

There was no longer any doubt in my mind: Harry was involved in Crawford's death. Maybe nobody could come up with any hard evidence, but he was involved. Given Harry's volatile emotional state, would he break

down under police questioning? But for that to happen
Larry Keller had to have a good reason to haul the young
man in. Maybe I could provoke Harry into doing something foolish. I caught Joe glancing at his watch.

"If you stick around, you can speak to him yourself.
Harry took Tweety-Bird up but he should be back in ten,
fifteen minutes."

"Tweety-Bird?"

Joe grinned. "That's what he calls his single-engine
Cessna. He keeps it at the Westport Flight Club."

I simply stared at Joe. It hadn't even occurred to me
that Harry could be a pilot. *Some investigator,* I thought,
disgusted with myself. Having access to a plane changed
everything. Harry could have flown the Cessna to a
small airport in Chicago, such as Meigs, established an
alibi with Thelma Young, left Orchestra Hall immediately after that, taken a cab to the airport, flown back
to Westport, shot his stepfather, clobbered me over the
head when I showed up unexpectedly, and returned to
Chicago in time to reclaim the Ferrari from the parking
garage at eleven-thirty.

I felt ill. Then the cold-bloodedness of the scheme
hit me and made me furious. Fighting my anger, I asked
Joe to give Harry a message from me.

"I'll be happy to pass on anything you want me to."

"Tell him that I know all about The Dolphin." Noting
Joe's perplexed expression, I added, "Harry'll know
what I mean. Believe me." I thanked him for his help
and stalked off. As soon as I got home, I called Uncle
Barney and told him what I'd found out.

"His own plane, huh? Well, I'll be. I didn't think of

that either, but then it's not as if every college kid could pilot a plane, much less own one."

"Do you think I did right by mentioning The Dolphin?"

"It might prod somebody into doing something rash, which is what we want. I think it's time to put a couple of people under surveillance. I'll let you know what shift I want you to take."

"How about checking out the small airports?"

"I'll put Glenn on that. You've done enough for a Sunday. Enjoy the rest of the weekend, Cybil."

I tried to do that, but didn't quite succeed. I felt uneasy and jumpy, expecting something to happen. Since I couldn't sit still long enough to listen to music or to read, I put on my work gloves and started to strip off the uglier-than-sin wallpaper above the chair railing in the dining room.

GLENN'S PRELIMINARY INVESTIGATION on Sunday had netted nothing except the information that Harry hadn't taken Tweety-Bird up on the Saturday Ariosto had been killed. I hadn't expected him to be so careless as to use his own plane.

On Monday morning Barney looked at the list of small airports in a hundred-mile radius of Westport and assigned one to each investigator. Mine turned out to be a surprisingly large airfield located west of the city just over the countyline. The receptionist directed me to a hangar where the manager-owner worked on some dial in the cockpit of a plane named Lily-Oh II.

"Mr. Dawson, could I speak to you for a minute?"

He raised his head. "Sure."

Dawson swung himself out of the cockpit with the grace of a gymnast. He was tall, lean, and long-legged. When he came closer the countless lines crisscrossing his weathered face belied the youthfulness of his movements. The World War II leather bomber jacket he wore looked like the real thing, though I suspected he wasn't old enough to have been a flyer in that war. When I told him what I needed to know, it turned out he knew Harry.

"Nobody took a plane up that Saturday night. The weather was bad. Rainy and windy," he said.

"Could anyone have gone up despite the weather?"

"Yeah. Somebody with lots of experience. Or a natural-born flier."

"Is Harry one of these natural-born fliers?"

"He sure is. Too bad his old man nixed the boy's aspirations to join the Air Force. Harry wanted to run away and sign up when he hit eighteen, but I encouraged him to go to college, graduate, and then join up. In the meantime he logged as much flying time as he could."

"How did Harry acquire his plane since Mr. Ariosto was opposed to him flying?"

"He used the money his mother left him. Ariosto had a fit, but there was nothing the old man could do about it. Tweety-Bird had been bought and paid for."

"You're sure Harry didn't take one of your planes that evening?"

"Positive. I was here till midnight. I wanted to stick around to turn the clocks back from daylight savings time. Then I went for a beer at Lynn's Tavern which is

just down the road a piece, parallel to the runway. I'd
have heard any plane taking off or landing."

I believed him, thanked him for his time, and left.

From my car I phoned the agency. Uncle Barney had
heard from the other investigators. Harry had not used a
plane that night. At least not in the tri-county area that
would have enabled him to shoot Ariosto and establish
his alibi in Chicago.

"So, that's that," I murmured, feeling defeated.

"For the moment. We'll examine all the facts again
and look for what we missed or misinterpreted," Barney
said. "Are you coming in?"

"In a little while. Since it's on the way, I'll stop at the
Ariosto mansion. I have the nagging feeling that I've
overlooked something important."

I had no idea what I could have missed, but it bothered me enough to pay the family another visit.

As soon as Brazier opened the door, I was hit with
the noise of unusual activity. Cartons were stacked three
high in the hall outside the study.

"What's going on?" I asked Brazier.

"Miss Annette has put Mr. Ramsey in charge of
everything."

Looking at Brazier's face closely, I couldn't detect
anything, and yet I was sure I'd perceived a hint of disapproval. "Are you staying on?"

"No, ma'am!"

This time the butler didn't hide his emotion. Brazier
might as well have shouted that nothing on earth could
induce him to serve Ramsey.

"Is Miss Annette here?"

"No. She had to fly to Detroit but she'll be back tomorrow."

"Oh. Then I'd like to talk to Mrs. Dougherty for a minute."

"She's in the kitchen. I know she'll be glad to see you."

Brazier's gloomy expression and tone of voice hurried me to the back of the house where I found a red-eyed Mrs. Dougherty moving through the kitchen aimlessly, wringing her hands. She was so discomposed that she allowed me to make the tea. Only after I had settled her into her favorite chair and dosed her cup liberally with sugar was she able to tell me what was wrong.

"He fired me, that's what's the matter. After all these years, he fired me!"

"Who fired you?"

"Mr. Ramsey. But I told him I had already retired, so he couldn't sack me. Imagine the nerve of that upstart! Offering me two months' salary and showing me the gate!"

Her shelf-like bosom heaved in agitation. "When did all this happen?"

"The lawyer came yesterday and announced that Miss Annette put Mr. Ramsey in charge of everything."

"I suppose that makes sense," I murmured. "She lives in Detroit and Harry is too young and inexperienced to take over."

"Well, he finally got what he always wanted."

"Who?"

"Mr. Ramsey. More than once I heard him hint around that he wanted to live here at the mansion but Mr. Ariosto wouldn't have him."

"Why not? Surely there was room for one more."

"Room to spare."

"Then why?"

Mrs. Dougherty shrugged. "Mr. Ariosto must have had his reasons. I only know that Mr. Ramsey's two-faced. Oh, he was always polite to us, the servants I mean, in front of people, but he treated us like dirt when no one was watching."

Maxi, speaking of the exemplary employers she had followed to the United States in her youth, said that the true test of someone's character was revealed in their relationship to servants or employees.

"Anyway, my sister's coming this afternoon to pick me up. I can't wait to leave this house," Mrs. Dougherty said.

I wondered what Pauline was going to do. Had Ramsey thrown her out too? I stayed with Mrs. Dougherty long enough to calm her down and listen to her plans for her retirement. After promising to keep in touch, I hugged her goodbye. Then I set out to find Pauline.

Ramsey's voice stopped me as I passed the study.

"What are you doing here, Cybil?" he asked, coming to the open door. He was carrying the small landscape painting that had hung behind the desk.

Determined to keep my eyes off the floor in front of the desk even though all traces of blood had been removed, I said, "I dropped by to see Pauline."

"She's in the morning room."

"I understand congratulations are in order."

Ramsey smiled. "Yeah. You're looking at the director of Ariosto Enterprises."

"And owner of this house?"

"No. Just the caretaker."

I sensed he would have loved to own the house. Ramsey already acted like the lord of the manor. "You're not wasting any time redecorating the place," I said, looking pointedly at the painting. He didn't even have the grace to look embarrassed.

"Terrance had no taste where art was concerned. Look at this kitsch."

"I've seen worse," I said.

"There's a phone call for you," Pauline told me, joining us.

"You can take it in here." Ramsey gestured towards the desk in the study.

It was Uncle Barney. I listened, not wanting to hear or believe what he had to say. "Are you sure?" I asked, knowing in my heart he would be. "Sweet heaven above," I murmured, replacing the receiver.

"Are you okay?" Ramsey asked.

"You look as pale as a ghost," Pauline said.

"Harry's plane crashed. He's dead," I blurted out.

FOURTEEN

PAULINE DIDN'T UTTER A SOUND. Her eyes rolled back in her head and before I could so much as open my mouth to speak, she crumpled to the floor like a rag doll.

"What the hell!" Ramsey yelled.

Both of us kneeled beside the still figure. I searched for her pulse, reassured when I located its beat.

"Pauline," I called. When she didn't respond, I unfastened the wide belt of her dress. "Ramsey, get me that pillow from the couch." After he did, I placed it under her feet.

"Does that help?" he asked.

"It's supposed to. Allows the blood to flow back to her heart."

"Pauline," Ramsey called to her.

She moaned. Her eyes fluttered open. They focused on me and she remembered. "No," she whispered through pale lips. "Tell me it's not true."

"I wish I could."

"Harry isn't dead. He can't be. No!"

The word became a long wail of agony that cut right through me. I was sure it could be heard in the far reaches of the mansion. Pauline rolled over onto her stomach, beating her fists against the wooden floor.

"Let her be," I told Ramsey, who tried to restrain her. I knew from experience that sometimes emotional torment can be borne only if it's matched by physical pain. "Get Brazier to phone her physician. She'll need a tranquilizer to get through this."

After a few minutes Pauline's screams dulled into a heartbroken keening that was even more terrible to hear. I stroked her hair, unable to murmur the traditional, meaningless phrases that I knew too well could bring her no comfort in her loss. When the first terrible wave of her pain receded momentarily, Pauline turned to look at me.

"How did it happen?" she asked between sobs.

The investigator assigned to shadow Harry had witnessed the crash, so I knew. When I hesitated, Pauline again demanded to know how her lover had died.

"According to several witnesses, the plane nose-dived to earth and exploded on impact." Though the words were brutally frank, the truth was usually less devastating than the images the mind invents if allowed to speculate. Pauline stared at me, trying to absorb this information, her tears stilled for the moment. Then what little color was left in her face drained away. She swayed. I grabbed her by the shoulders and shook her.

"Pauline, don't you dare faint again," I ordered. Although losing consciousness is a natural response to great shock, it still scared me.

"He killed himself. My Harry killed himself. He said he might, but I thought I'd talked him out of it. It's my fault. All my fault. Oh, my sweet, sweet Harry."

She began to sob, great gasping sobs that shook her body. Pauline collapsed against me. I held her until Ramsey returned.

"Her doctor said he'd prescribed Valium for her already. Brazier went to get it."

Moments later Brazier returned with the prescription bottle and a glass of water. I read the instructions, noting that I could give her two pills. Pauline was crying so hard it took both Brazier and myself to get her to swallow the pills before we persuaded her to rest on the sofa. Then I pulled up a chair beside her and sat down.

I don't know whether the pills started to take effect quickly or whether Pauline was too exhausted to continue to weep, but a curious resignation settled over her. She began to speak in a soft voice.

"It's all my fault, all of it. Harry didn't do anything wrong except help me move him. I kept telling Harry not to worry. I'd take the blame, but it bothered him so badly he could hardly eat or sleep."

Suddenly I knew what she was talking about. "Harry didn't shoot Crawford, did he?"

"No. He only helped me move the body. I phoned him. I didn't know what else to do."

"Where did you shoot Crawford?"

"In the park. Down by the river where he always met me to collect the money."

"He was blackmailing you?"

Pauline nodded. "He found out about Harry and me. By a stupid coincidence. We were so careful except for that one time. After the Tri State picnic at Lake Michigan, we didn't go home to switch cars. It seemed so dumb to drive to Westport when we were practically at the motel already. Crawford saw Harry's Ferrari and my Mercedes pull off the highway and followed us."

"From whom did Harry borrow the mustang?" I asked to satisfy my curiosity.

"From his roommate."

"Why did you shoot Crawford?"

"Because I was desperate. He demanded more and more money. I couldn't come up with any more. I probably would have started to pawn my jewelry and continued to pay him, but he taunted me. He laughed and called me names and then he hit me. I guess I panicked. I grabbed the shotgun and pulled the trigger."

"Why did you take the gun with you? No, maybe you'd better not answer that," I added, conscious of Ramsey standing behind me. Her answer could prove premeditation and that was something I didn't want to have to report to the police. Making a conviction stick wasn't part of my job.

"It doesn't matter," she continued, her whole body acknowledging defeat. "Without Harry nothing matters anymore."

"The gun," Ramsey reminded her.

"It was in the car. I'd just been to the Sports Club. I'd taken it to the gunsmith there to check. I never meant to shoot Crawford."

"Why didn't you leave the body there and call the police? With Crawford hitting you, it would have been self-defense," I said.

"I didn't think. I drove to the nearest phone and called Harry. He came and we decided to put the body into the conference room. We didn't think it would be found before Monday. Maybe not till Tuesday. That would have given us time to decide what to do."

"You could still have told the police after they found the body."

"We thought about doing that, but then the gun disappeared from the rack, and we didn't know what to do."

"When did you notice that the gun was gone?"

"On Monday afternoon. That's when I ordered the replacement just as you guessed."

"Pauline, think carefully. Who was in the house from the time on Sunday evening when you put the gun back into the rack and Monday afternoon when you noticed its disappearance?"

"Don't you think you should let her rest?" Ramsey asked.

"In a little bit. Think, Pauline. Who else was in the house?"

"Everybody in the family. Harry, Terrance, Ramsey, and me. And all the staff."

That didn't help much. "Did Sidney Dunn blackmail you?"

"Yes. But not until after Terrance was shot. He found out about Harry and me. I don't know how he got the key to the motel room. He was an awful snoop, so it wasn't hard for him to find things."

"Did you shoot Sidney?"

"No. When I heard you say he'd been shot, I thought Harry might have shot him. But when I'd had time to think, I knew he couldn't have."

"And you didn't shoot your husband either, did you?" I asked.

"Shoot Terrance? Heavens, no. I was much too afraid

of the man to pull a gun on him. Besides, I didn't have the shotgun anymore. And Harry didn't either."

I believed her. "What were you and Harry planning to do?"

"We were going to run off together as soon as Harry graduated. We never planned to fall in love. It just happened. We both tried to fight it. We really did. You've got to believe me, Cybil."

"I do." I could see her eyes grow heavy. "Sleep now," I murmured.

"Harry," she whispered. Tears trickled silently down her cheek even as she fell asleep.

I rose from the chair, feeling as if I'd been through the proverbial wringer.

"You believe she didn't kill Terrance and the chauffeur?" Ramsey asked.

"Yes. Don't you?"

"No way. She killed all three men."

His certainty and the barely suppressed satisfaction I detected in his voice appalled me. I clamped my teeth together and counted to ten. Brazier's return saved me from an argument that could easily have become ugly.

"Mrs. Quindt, could you look in on Mrs. Dougherty? She's mighty upset over Mr. Harry's death."

"I'll go see her right now."

I found Mrs. Dougherty sitting at the kitchen table, her face buried in her hands. "I'm so sorry. I know how fond you were of Harry." I laid my hand on her shoulder.

Looking up with tears in her eyes, she said, "My poor lamb. He never had a chance. Not with a woman like her."

"You knew about the affair?"

"I suspected it."

"Did anyone else?" I asked.

She shook her head. "I don't think so. I only suspected because I've known Harry since he was a little boy. He never could hide things from me."

Taking a deep breath, I said, "Mrs. Dougherty, we still don't know who killed Mr. Ariosto. Now that Pauline has confessed to killing Crawford, everybody will try to blame her for the other two deaths as well. That will implicate Harry."

"No! Harry is innocent. He could never kill anyone. There isn't a mean bone in his body. I mean, there wasn't." She pressed her hand over her mouth to keep back the sobs.

"I think he is innocent, too, but I need your help to prove that. Think back to that Sunday night and Monday morning. Who was in and out of the house?"

"This will help my boy?"

"Yes."

Mrs. Dougherty wiped her eyes with a tissue and blew her nose. Then she was ready. "Well, let me see. On Sundays we have the main meal at noon, so I don't have to cook in the evening. I just make sure there are plenty of snacks and sandwich fixings in the refrigerator."

I let her tell it in her own way, hoping this method would best trigger her memory.

"After I got back from visiting my sister, Mr. Ariosto asked me to fix him a turkey sandwich, which I did. Then Mr. Ramsey arrived and joined Mr. Ariosto in the study. He stayed there until Mrs. Ariosto and Harry came. They didn't want anything from the kitchen. Just drinks from the bar."

"Did Mr. Ariosto join them?"

"No. Only Mr. Ramsey. Later I heard them go out and Mrs. Ariosto came back in."

"Did all three go out at the same time?"

"No. Mr. Ramsey left a couple of minutes earlier. Let's see. Where was I? Oh yes. Sunday evening. When the police called, Mr. Ariosto went to the warehouse."

"What did Mrs. Ariosto do?"

"When she came in after seeing Harry off, she went straight upstairs."

"Did Mr. Ariosto tell everyone that Crawford had been killed when he returned?"

"Brazier, Sidney, and I were sitting in the kitchen. Mr. Ariosto came in and told us. Then he said he was going to phone Mr. Ramsay with the news."

"Tell me about Monday."

"Mr. Ariosto got up early as always, had a light breakfast, and left. Mrs. Ariosto got up early too, which was unusual. Harry came home."

"Wasn't that unusual, too?"

Mrs. Dougherty shrugged. "He said he left a book here."

"Did he talk to Mrs. Ariosto?"

"Yes. They went for a walk together. I saw them from the kitchen window. No sooner had they gone, when Mr. Ramsey arrived, saying he forgot some papers. You want me to go on with who was here for lunch?"

"No, that's not necessary. Thank you."

"I hope this helps clear my poor lamb."

"It will." Mrs. Dougherty's face brightened.

Now I knew who killed Terrance Ariosto and Sidney Dunn. I even had an inkling what the motive in the Ariosto murder was and how the alibi had been rigged, but I had absolutely no tangible proof. Zero. Zilch. Uncle Barney claims that there's no such thing as a perfect crime. The perpetrator always makes at least one mistake, even if a very small one. Obviously I had to find it. I wasn't about to let Pauline be accused of committing two premeditated murders.

On my way to the study to check on Pauline, I met Ramsey.

"I phoned Annette. She's taking the next flight. She was pretty broken up about Harry."

Why that should surprise him, I couldn't imagine. After all, Annette had known and cared for Harry since he was a boy. She'd stood up for him, even to her father.

"I also called the police."

"You didn't waste any time, did you," I snapped, not hiding my annoyance. "Pauline's just had a tremendous shock. Couldn't you have waited?"

"Why? She'll have to face the authorities sooner or later. You want a drink, Cybil?"

"No, thank you."

"I think I'll have one."

I waited until Ramsey entered the study before I hurried into the game room. Standing before the gun rack, I wondered how the murderer had smuggled the shotgun out of the house. Uncle Barney suspected that he'd hidden it under his raincoat when he came to kill Ariosto. Could he have smuggled it out the same way? In broad daylight on Monday morning with people coming and going? If he had nerves of steel he could and there was no hint that the killer lacked those.

I crossed to the nearest of the two windows. Both faced the rose garden. Unlatching the window, I noticed that it opened soundlessly and that the screen was the type that could be removed by pulling out two screws on each side, something that took mere seconds. It would be a cinch to lower the gun out the window and pick it up on the way to the car, a raincoat casually thrown over it.

Where was the murder weapon? Scrutinizing the shotguns again, I realized that their size alone eliminated many of the most common hiding places. He could have thrown it into the river. If he had, we could never prove he committed those murders. But if Sidney saw him take the gun from the house, the murderer might have been reluctant to risk being seen with the weapon again.

The impatient, authoritative pounding on the front door could only mean one thing: Sam Keller and his men had arrived.

Sam took one look at Pauline before storming back to the living room where Ramsey and I waited.

"Who gave her the sedative?" Sam bellowed.

"I did."

"I might have known it was you, Cybil."

"We had her physician's permission," I told him. "Besides, a couple of hours can't make much difference to you, but they will help Pauline.

"What if she recants her confession when she wakes up feeling better?"

"She won't. But even if she did, you're no worse off

than before." I could see Sam struggle with his temper. In the end he merely glowered at me.

"Who all heard the confession?"

"Ramsey, Brazier, and I."

"And she confessed to all three murders?"

"She did not!" I shot Ramsey a slit-eyed look. He had obviously intimated that over the telephone. "She only admitted shooting Crawford and from what she said, she acted in self-defense."

"Is that what you heard, too?" Sam asked Ramsey.

"More or less. If you believe Pauline."

"You don't?"

Ramsey shrugged. "She's a clever woman. She probably figured you'd nail her for the Crawford murder so she confessed, hoping to get away with pleading self-defense. Or maybe she thought if she owned up to one murder, you'd forget about the other two."

"That's pure bilge, and you know it," I told Ramsey. "Pauline didn't have to confess at all. The police weren't exactly breathing down her neck."

"Calm down, Cybil," Sam said. "Nobody is going to railroad anybody. However, it's a fact that all three men were killed with the same gun which strongly points to the murderer being the same person. Even you thought that."

"Up till now. Pauline says the gun was stolen. Probably that Monday morning. I believe her. She isn't lying, not when she feels the way she does."

"And how's that?" Sam asked.

"That she's got nothing left to lose."

Ramsey snorted. "Nothing left to lose? Only her

freedom. Possibly her life." His voice resounded with sarcasm.

"I didn't realize you disliked Pauline that much, Ramsey."

"I don't, but I'm not taken in by her dramatics."

"I'd hardly describe losing somebody you love as dramatics." I could feel red-hot anger rise in me.

Sam stepped between us, addressing me. "Tell me about the gun being stolen."

I told him about Pauline charging the purchase of a replacement.

"That doesn't prove anything either way. We've got to find that gun," Sam muttered.

"Do you still need me here?" I asked.

"No. You can go, but come by the station later so we can take your statement. You won't forget, will you?"

"I'll be there."

In the hall I nodded to Sergeant Griffin who leaned against the wall opposite the study, keeping an eye on Pauline.

I drove straight to the airport, the nearest place that had what I needed. First I telephoned Uncle Barney. I ended my report with a request. "I want a tail on Ramsey Ariosto right away."

"I thought you cleared him," Barney said.

"I did. Now I have to destroy that alibi I worked so hard to build for him. What makes me absolutely furious is that he played me as if I were a fish at the end of his line. Pretending not to remember the girl who sold him the cookies the first time I interviewed him. Ha! He knew damned well his alibi would look stronger if I established it than if he told it to me or the police. Ramsey used me, and that's something I can't stand!"

"Calm down, Cybil."

It irked me that everybody was telling me to calm down when I really didn't feel like calming down. I wanted to yell at the top of my lungs. I wanted to throw things, like a stack of big, white stoneware plates against a cement wall. Since I didn't have plates handy and since I wouldn't dream of creating a scene by yelling, I took several deep hatha yoga breaths.

"I'm calm," I said through half-clenched teeth. "If Ramsey hasn't ditched the murder weapon yet, I strongly suspect he'll try to get rid of it the first chance he gets. I want one of us to catch him in the act."

"I'll assign someone to shadow him. Where's Ramsey now?"

"At the mansion. I'm sure he's going to stay there until Pauline is arrested and taken to jail, the whole time trying to persuade Sam that she's guilty of all three murders."

"Where'll you be?"

"As soon as I rent a car, I'll watch the mansion from Locust Road. Ramsey's Chrysler Imperial is visible from there, so that's where I'll park."

I rented an inconspicuous beige Chevy, left my Volvo in the airport's long-term parking lot, and took Locust Road to the side street nearest the Ariosto estate. It was really just a lane but wide enough for a car to get past me. Ramsey's car was still parked in the same spot. As I waited for the operative from the agency to arrive, I tried to come up with a plan of action.

After a while I got out of the car and paced. By the

time Glenn's Toyota parked behind me, I knew what I had to do.

On the phone Mrs. Taylor agreed to see me if I could get to her house before one when she took her daughters back to St. Mary's Elementary School. I told her I would be there in half an hour. I beat that by four minutes.

"I hope you don't mind talking while I fix lunch for the girls," she said, leading the way to the kitchen.

"I don't mind."

The counters and appliances were arranged in a U-shape with the kitchen table placed in the open part of the U. The girls, sitting at the table side by side, cast curious but shy glances at me from time to time, while their mother sliced Spam into a frying pan.

"Mrs. Taylor, you said you knew what time it was when you picked up your daughter by looking at Mr. Ariosto's wall clock. Did you look at any other clock when you arrived home?"

"No. I went straight to the kitchen to decorate the cupcakes. As you can see, my clock on the range doesn't work. My husband keeps promising to fix it but something else always comes up."

"Did you listen to the radio in the car or in the kitchen?"

"No. Nancy always listens to loud music and the girls have the television on full blast. Frankly, I enjoy the quiet."

"So, your only source of information on time was Mr. Ariosto's clock?"

"Yes. Until we went to bed and I set the alarm. I'm not real hung up on time," she confided, dividing the fried Spam between two plates. She added two slices of white bread and placed the plates before her daughters. Mrs. Taylor uncapped a bottle of ketchup, upended it and hit the bottom. She paused, wrinkling her forehead. "You know, later on that evening I was surprised how much I'd gotten done by nine. Was Mr. Ariosto's clock wrong?"

"Something like that," I said evasively. Mrs. Taylor would undoubtedly be called to testify, so I was careful not to put words into her mouth. "Thank you for your time. Please stay. I can find my own way out." I left her trying to dislodge the ketchup from the bottle.

Before returning to the office I used the drive-through of the nearest fast food restaurant to pick up a hamburger with lettuce and tomato and a small soft drink.

Lynn, looking stunning in a crimson charmeuse tunic over black pants, frowned at my carry-in lunch. She thinks eating at my desk isn't upscale enough for the image she wants the agency to project. I ignored the frown, wishing I could wear that shade of red without looking completely washed out.

Fifteen minutes later I met with Uncle Barney.

"I talked to Sam. Pauline Ariosto has been arrested for the murder of Galen Crawford," Barney told me.

"He didn't waste any time, did he? Did Sam say anything about the other murders?"

"Just the standard reply: they're following leads."

Which meant they'd be questioning Pauline until she dropped.

"Don't look so unhappy, Cybil. The Westport police do not use rubber hoses. Besides, Pauline has an attorney to protect her rights."

Barney mentioned the law firm which was prestigious enough, but their expertise didn't extend to criminal proceedings, I thought.

"They'll bring in some big name criminal lawyer before the trial, I'm sure," he added. "What did you find out this morning?"

I told him about my visit to Mrs. Taylor.

"You think Ramsey set the clock ahead?"

"Yes. When Mrs. Taylor came to pick up her daughter, it was only six forty-five, not seven forty-five. That gave him time to get to the Ariosto estate and back. If she had commented on the time difference, he could have claimed to be confused about the imminent daylight savings standard time change. He was lucky. Since it was a rainy day, it was dark out, so Mrs. Taylor accepted the time shown on Ramsey's fancy clock. He took a chance and it worked."

"You're convinced Ramsey shot Ariosto and Dunn?"

"Yes. If you'd seen and heard Pauline, you would have believed her, too. She admits shooting Crawford in self-defense. From what Cathy said about him, he had a reputation for being rough with women."

Barney fiddled with his pipe. After a while he said, as if thinking aloud, "Harry is dead. Sidney is dead. You've ruled out Annette. That leaves Ramsey. He had opportunity and motive which I think was greed. Would you agree with that?"

"Yes. Greed and love of power. You should have observed him at the mansion. He loves running the whole show. But I don't think his motive was only greed. Something else happened. Something in his relationship with his uncle contradicts Ramsey's claim that he and Terrance were close. If that had been the case, why would Terrance have refused to allow his nephew to live on the estate? That building is big enough to house a dozen people without crowding anyone."

"Mrs. Taylor's testimony won't be enough to bring him to trial unless we come up with some additional proof, preferably physical proof," Barney pointed out.

"I know. If only we could find that blasted gun." We were both silent, thinking about this problem. Suddenly I remembered something. "Pauline said she'd taken the gun to the gunsmith at the Sports Club. I think I'll talk to him."

"You might as well. Maybe he'll know something we can use to trace it."

I phoned the Sports Club. The gunsmith, Mr. Mueller, was on the shooting range but was expected to be in his workshop shortly. I left a message, stating that I would be there by two-thirty to pick up a gun he had repaired. I was fairly certain that this would get me into the club without trouble.

MR. MUELLER WAS A BEAR of a man. Not only was he physically huge, he was hairy. He'd tied his long black hair with a thick leather thong. His sideburns met the bushy beard that hid his lower face.

"What can I do for you?" His voice rumbled from his deep chest.

"Mrs. Pauline Ariosto brought in a shotgun for you to look at. What can you tell me about that?"

"It was her favorite shotgun. I gave it a general tune-up so to speak."

"What's distinctive about Mrs. Ariosto's gun? How could I identify it among a whole rack of similar shotguns?"

He worked his fingers through his beard, thinking. Then he grinned. "It's got a nick in the stock. It's a tiny nick, but big enough to make it stand out from other guns."

"Where on the stock?" I asked, hardly daring to believe this lucky break.

The gunsmith picked up a gun and showed me. "Run your hand over the butt plate like this and just onto the stock. You can't see the nick unless you know what you're looking for, but you can sure feel it."

"Would you be willing to repeat this to the police and in a court of law?"

Mueller looked alarmed, but that didn't mean he was necessarily guilty of anything. Most people were not too eager to face the police.

"Will it help Mrs. Ariosto?" he asked.

"Yes."

"Then I will. She has a real appreciation for a fine gun. Don't find too many women like that."

I thanked him profusely.

At last we were getting some place. Not that I knew where to start looking for the gun, but at least I'd know when I found it. That was not quite true, I realized with a start. I knew exactly where to start the search. He might no longer have the gun. On the other hand, he was arrogant and cocky and a shotgun wasn't as easy to get rid of as a handgun. In any event, a search was definitely in order.

I took a deep breath to tame the butterflies cavorting in my stomach. What I was about to do was just a tad risky.

FIFTEEN

DRIVING THROUGH THE PARKING LOT of Ramsey's apartment complex, I searched for his slot. Although I'd been fairly certain he wouldn't be home yet, I had to make sure. I parked the rented Chevy in the visitors' lot. Palming the skeleton keys, I sauntered casually to the back door of his building. In a complex almost exclusively occupied by young professionals, four o'clock in the afternoon is dead time which suited my purpose perfectly. Even so, I quickly glanced in all directions before I tried the door. It was unlocked.

I met no one as I walked up the flight of stairs or in the hall, but passing the apartment next to Ramsey's, I heard piano music. Chopin, I thought. Praying that occupant would stay put for the rest of the prelude, I studied Ramsey's lock. The second key I tried opened the door. I slipped inside quickly and found myself in total darkness.

In his haste to take custody of the Ariosto mansion that morning, Ramsey had left all the drapes closed. Chastising myself for not bringing a flashlight, I decided it was quicker to turn on some lights than to open all the drapes. Hopefully no one would notice if a little light spilled out from beneath doors and around windows. Adjusting the surgical gloves I had borrowed from

Luke's emergency supply, I glanced around, looking for places he could have hidden the shotgun.

Before I searched any of the rooms, I thought it best to make a quick survey of the entire apartment. Remembering the kitchen, I merely swept it with a brief glance. There was no sign of the cookie box he had used to dupe me. Ramsey Ariosto had spoiled chocolate chip cookies for me forever.

The navy-blue-and-white tiled bathroom featured a tub-shower combination and sleek Euro-style cabinets and washbasin. Unless he had put in a secret trap door, there was no space to hide a shotgun. On the way out I had to stop myself from automatically picking up the pile of wet towels on the floor.

Ramsey had left his king-size bed unmade, something Maxi considers the height of slovenliness. Naturally, I consequently never leave my bed unmade. One wall of the room consisted of floor-to-ceiling closets which would take some time to search.

The second bedroom served as a sort of den-cum-storage area for his sports equipment. I recognized the bow he'd used at the Sports Club. A golf bag rested in a corner next to tennis racquets, baseball bats and mitts, a jumble of shoes including basketball high tops, nylon running sneakers, and cleated baseball shoes. I could have imagined that. I turned and caught my breath. A gun rack, much like the one in the Ariosto game room, stood between two windows, holding three shotguns and a rifle.

Had Ramsey read "The Purloined Letter"? Was he clever and reckless enough to hide the murder weapon in plain view? There was only one way to find out. The gun cabinet was locked and being an antique, it wouldn't yield to the first half dozen keys I tried. I felt sweat bead on my forehead. The clock in the living room chimed the half hour. Four-thirty. As head honcho of Ariosto Enterprises, Ramsey could decide to come home early. That possibility sent my heart racing. Unfortunately, it also made my fingers tremble.

Closing my eyes in concentration, I willed my hands to become steady. Just when I was tempted to force the lock, my pick worked. The door to the gun cabinet opened with a click that sounded unnaturally loud.

I removed the shotgun, running my fingers over the butt plate and the stock as the gunsmith had showed me. Nothing. I checked again. The wood was smooth and unmarred. I replaced the gun and tried the next one. When the living room clock announced four forty-five, I paused for a moment, knowing I had to get out of the apartment. With almost feverish haste I examined the second gun. I couldn't believe that it, too, was unmarked. Could I have been wrong?

With some trepidation I reached for the last gun. The nick was there! Tiny, not easily visible, the damaged spot was exactly where Mr. Mueller said it would be.

"All right!" I murmured, feeling immense satisfaction. Now all that was left for me to do was tell Sam to come to the apartment with a search warrant. Carefully I set the gun back in its place. As I reached for the glass door to shut it, I thought I heard a noise in the living room. I froze, listening intently. My heart jumped into my throat, my blood roared in my ears when I heard the unmistakable click of the front door closing.

"What the hell…."

Ramsey's voice. I had left the lights on. He had to realize someone had been or was still in his apartment. Even though I knew there was no place to hide, my eyes frantically searched the room. His footsteps, though muffled by the carpet, closed in on me, trapping me.

Ramsey stopped in the open doorway, the revolver in his hand pointed at me. His eyes jumped to the half-opened cabinet and back to me. He knew, I thought, horrified.

"How'd you figure it out?"

"Figure what out?" I bluffed.

"Cut the crap, Cybil. Why else would you be looking at my guns except to find Pauline's? Step away from the gun rack."

To underscore his order, he motioned the gun in the direction he wanted me to go. I did as I was told, though I asked, "Are you afraid I'm going to jump you and take the revolver from you?"

Ramsey ignored that. Without taking his eyes off me, he shut the glass door. With his left hand he located a small key on the key ring he'd taken from his pocket and locked the cabinet.

"Who knows you're here?"

Ramsey was thinking about shooting me, I thought, not quite believing it.

"Answer me."

His gray eyes, cold and calculating, impaled me, and I knew he meant to kill me. Fear shot through me, paralyzing me. I couldn't even speak.

"So, nobody knows," he said, reading my reaction correctly. "Excellent. That'll make it so much simpler."

Ramsey's sarcastic remark roused me. I'd be damned

if I was going to make anything simple and easy for him. "Uncle Barney knows I'm here," I lied brazenly, looking him straight in the eye. My voice was surprisingly strong, lending credence to my claim. I knew he half believed me.

Ramsey shrugged. "It doesn't matter."

Glenn should be parked outside. Unless he lost Ramsey while tailing him, but that was highly unlikely. Somehow I had to get Ramsey outside. "You're not going to shoot me in here, are you? Your music-loving neighbor is bound to hear it. I know this particular prelude. It doesn't rise to the kind of shattering crescendo that would cover the sound of a shot." I could tell he was thinking this over.

"You're right. We'll wait until dark before we leave."

Reprieved for an hour or so.

"Walk into the living room and sit on the couch," he ordered.

I did. He perched on the edge of an easy chair, facing me, the revolver steady in his hand. A low coffee table stood between us. The only thing on it heavy enough to be used as a weapon was a large glass ashtray. I eyed it longingly. Ramsey would have to turn his head long enough for me to grab it, leap across the table and smash it on his head hard enough to stun him and wrest the gun away from him.

No, I didn't just want to stun him, I discovered. I wanted to put a large bump on his head. That would be poetic justice. Of course, the chances of my doing that were minimal. Once outside, they improved somewhat. Maybe we'd meet people coming home from work.

Maybe I could break away and run. Would he shoot me with witnesses around? I didn't think so.

But what if no one came? What if we were alone in the dark parking lot? What if he succeeded in forcing me to drive his car to a lonely spot where he'd raise the gun and… My mouth felt parched and dry, but the palms of my hands were damp. I'd have to take any chance I got, even a lousy one, before we reached his car.

"You never answered my question, Cybil. How did you tumble to me as the guilty party?"

"What?" It took me a moment to focus on his question. "Oh, that. Logic, I guess."

Ramsey frowned. "I don't understand. Explain."

"Pauline didn't shoot Terrance. That left you, so you had to have done it. It's perfectly clear and logical."

"I don't get it. Pauline could have been lying. How could you be so certain she was telling the truth?"

In her pain Pauline was beyond lies. The agony of her loss burned away all other emotions, all other concerns until nothing else existed but the shattering awareness of what she'd lost. But I knew Ramsey would not understand that, so I didn't bother to explain. All I said was, "Sometimes the truth is startlingly obvious."

Ramsey looked unconvinced.

"Why did you kill your uncle?" I wasn't sure Ramsey would answer that, but he did.

"Because I was tired of being jerked around like a yo-yo. I worked and slaved for that man but do you think he ever acknowledged my contribution? No way. And he never got tired of telling me how he took me in after my father died and raised me like his own son and how much money he'd spent on me. He repeated that over and over until I could recite it in my sleep. God protect us from that kind of charity. Well, that Friday it all came to a head. I told him that I more than repaid him with years of had work. Do you know what he had the gall to do?"

I shook my head, afraid that if I spoke Ramsey would stop his confession.

"He gave a position that he'd dangled in front of me like a carrot, a position he'd promised me, to someone else. Can you believe that? For two years I've worked my tail off in hopes of getting the vice presidency, and he gave it away. Just like that." He paused, as if he still couldn't believe what had happened.

"Not that the guy who got it was any better than me. Far from it. He wasn't nearly as qualified. No, Terrance did it for the sheer pleasure of tormenting me. Nothing gave him the charge that besting someone or doing someone in did, not even sex. Giving that job to someone else killed two birds with one stone: Terrance knew it would eat away at me, and it gave him a new victim in the newly promoted guy. The man couldn't possibly handle the job, and Terrance knew it. Terrance Ariosto was the biggest bastard that ever lived. He deserved to die."

"So, when Crawford was shot you saw your chance. How did you find out about Pauline and Harry's involvement?"

"That was easy. I saw them come in that Sunday and knew something drastic had happened. So I waited outside for them and overheard enough to know what had happened when Terrance told me about Crawford's death."

"How did you know about the shotgun?"

"I saw Pauline with it at the Sports Club that afternoon. I came back to the house on Monday and took it."

"That's when Dunn saw you?"

"That damned snoop. He saw me carry something to my car. He must have seen the empty spot in the gun rack and put two and two together. Blackmail is about as low as you can sink."

Personally, I thought murder deserved that distinction, but I wasn't about to argue with a man pointing a big revolver at me who'd already killed twice.

"It was you who hit me over the head in the study?"

"Yeah. You arrived a couple of minutes too early. I was at the house in the morning and found out that Terrance was going to be alone that evening. I didn't know he had asked you to join him. You almost wrecked everything."

There was actually an accusing note in his voice. I couldn't believe it. "Ah, but then I established an alibi for you. You must have enjoyed that."

"I did. You were wonderful. So earnest, so concerned, so eager to help."

Ramsey had the nerve to grin. At that moment I understood the urge to slug someone. I clenched my hands in helpless fury. Ramsey glanced at the clock on the wall. It wasn't time yet. I wasn't ready. I had to keep him talking.

"What was Terrance's reaction when you pointed the shotgun at him?" I asked.

"He laughed at first, claiming I'd never have the guts

to shoot him. What was so funny about that was that in my fantasies I'd killed the bastard a thousand times."

I'd been wrong about one thing. It hadn't been a dispassionate murder. The suppressed anger and humiliation of a dozen years had fired that shot. A shiver ran down my spine.

"Let's go. It's dark enough."

Startled, I looked into his eyes. Cold determination had replaced the feverish emotions I'd seen there moments earlier.

"For what it's worth, Cybil, I never intended to hurt you," Ramsey said. He stood up, the gun steady in his hand.

"But a man's got to do what a man's got to do?"

"Something like that. Move it, Cybil."

I was still afraid, terribly afraid, but anger coursed through me and with it came the determination to thwart Ramsey. I was not going to be a meek victim. I'd put up one hell of a fight, and I would win.

The hall was empty. Passing his neighbor's door, I noticed that Chopin had been replaced with a piece from the Renaissance. Not Vivaldi, but a contemporary of his. With a gun pressed against the small of my back, that was an odd thing for me to notice.

Nearing the door to the parking lot, I tensed for action. Glenn was somewhere out there, but probably too far to help me. I was on my own. I stopped, waiting for Ramsey to open the door. When he did, I gained two steps on him. The moment I set foot on the brightly lit landing, I cast a quick look around. Two women approached us. Without hesitation and without warning, I flung myself forward and rolled down the three steps.

"Oh my God. Are you hurt?" one of the women shrieked, rushing to my side.

"My ankle. I'm sure I've broken it," I cried out piteously.

"Are you sure?" the other woman asked.

"My husband is Dr. Luke Quindt. He's in charge of the emergency services at Westport Hospital so I know something about these things." The more information about me I could reveal before Ramsey forced me to go with him, the better my chances of survival were. I groaned for effect. Several other people joined the circle around me, I noticed, pleased. The bigger the crowd, the better. Ramsey faded farther to the rear.

"Cybil? Please let me through."

"Glenn?"

"I saw you fall. Are you okay?" Glenn squatted beside me.

In a voice no one but he could hear I said, "I'm fine. Do you see Ramsey?"

Glenn glanced around. "No. I saw him come through the door behind you, but I don't see him now."

"Good. Help me up. We have to make an urgent phone call."

TWO HOURS LATER, after Sam had removed the shotgun from Ramsey's apartment, after he'd taken my statement and had put out an all-points bulletin, we learned from the highway patrol that Ramsey Ariosto had run a road-block in Michigan. He had been killed instantly.

I went home then. The house was empty and quiet. I longed for company, but it was too late to disturb Maxi. Luke? I was tempted, but if I called him, he would expect more than being merely a sympathetic listener. I wasn't ready to be what he expected me to be.

I fixed a pot of Darjeeling tea, lit a fire, and listened to Beethoven's Ninth Symphony. Eventually the music washed away the dregs of fear and horror that still clung to me.

BECAUSE OF THE CASE, I had missed going to the cemetery on All Saints' Day. It's an Austrian custom to honor the dead with a visit on this day, a custom Maxi has always kept. I bought a huge bouquet of mums which I divided and added to the ones Maxi had already placed on the graves of our dead: my son's, my father's, my grandfather's and my Aunt Elise's, Maxi's daughter whom polio took in the early fifties.

I kept one perfectly petaled white blossom for Wilma. Though she wasn't a member of my family, I had liked her.

Although the caretaker had given me directions, it took me a while to find Wilma's marker. I stood before it, remembering her: quick, efficient, friendly and unfailingly cheerful except for the one time when the Carnes, mother and son, had been mentioned.

My breath caught. I recalled Maxi's words. She had been truly surprised that Tom had escaped his mother's overpowering hold long enough to get married. I added Cathy's description of the mother-son relationship to Maxi's. What emerged was the portrait of an unhealthily strong attachment. What would happen if such an attachment was suddenly severed?

Suddenly I knew, though again I didn't have a shred of evidence, only my suppositions.

Then I remembered something Ferne Lauder had said. I telephoned her from my car. After the usual exchange of greetings, I asked, "Do you remember the day my uncle and I came to talk to you?"

"Of course, I do. Not much happens around here, so I remember anything that's out of the ordinary."

"Good. I asked you then if you'd seen cars parked on the street that you hadn't seen there before."

"Yes. And I told you there hadn't been a Trans Am like my grandson's or a big Cadillac."

"But what had you seen?"

"A red jeep."

"I thought you'd said that, but I had to be sure."

"Does that help you, dear?"

"It does. Thanks a lot."

"Listen, why don't you come by some time for a beer?"

Hearing the loneliness in her voice, I said, "I will before the week is out." And I would go see her, but first I'd pick up a cold six-pack to take along.

A red jeep.

Flipping through the phone book I located the address I needed. It was near the cemetery. I saw the jeep sitting in the driveway from half a block away. I parked behind it. When I knocked, Cathy opened the door.

"My goodness. I didn't expect to see you again," she said. "I just got home from work. Come in."

"Thanks. Is Tom home?"

She stared at me with a mixture of alarm and surprise. "He's in the den. He hasn't been himself lately. Is something wrong? What's he done?"

"We'll let him tell us." I followed her to the den.

When I saw Tom, I was shocked. He looked shrunken, as if his clothes had grown too big for him. He seemed listless, barely looking at me when I greeted him.

"Cathy, I'd like you to stay," I said, sitting in a chair facing Tom. She sat beside him on the sofa.

"Maxi sends greetings. You remember her, don't you, Tom? She was your mother's friend," I said, my voice gentle as if I addressed a sick child.

He nodded indifferently.

"Do you also remember Wilma?" A change came over him. His eyes focused on me. I shrank from the exultant, triumphant expression gleaming in them.

"She's the one who drove the car that hurt Mama."

"So you decided to hurt her."

"Yes. Mama told me to."

"Tom, what are you talking about?" Cathy asked, horrified. "I can't believe Mae told you to—"

"—push Wilma down the stairs," I finished the sentence for her.

"She didn't tell me how to do it. The stairs were my idea."

Tom seemed to be proud of that.

"I don't believe your mother told you to kill Wilma," Cathy said, now as pale as the white wall behind her.

Tom turned on her. "That's how little you know. She told me every night until I did it. Now Mama can rest. The guilty have been punished."

Cathy and I stared at each other.

"Let me get this straight," Cathy said. "Mae talked to you after…after she died."

"Sure." Tom rubbed his temples as if he felt pain there. "I heard her voice every night until I pushed

Wilma down the stairs. Now everything's quiet." His hands fell away from his temples, resting relaxed in his lap. An almost angelic smile hovered around his lips.

"May I use your phone?" I asked Cathy.

"Sure. It's in the hall."

She joined me there just as I completed my call to the police.

"What'll happen to him?" Cathy asked, nodding her head in the direction of the den.

"The police are on their way. My guess is that he'll be placed in a mental institution."

Cathy sighed. "I knew he was growing weirder by the day, but I had no idea he'd done that to Wilma."

"It's not your fault," I reassured her, touching her arm.

She looked at me, her expression grateful. "Thanks. I needed to hear that."

After that there was nothing left to say. She returned to sit with her husband. I went outside and stood on the porch, waiting for the police.

REQUEST YOUR FREE BOOKS!

2 FREE NOVELS
PLUS 2 FREE GIFTS!

WORLDWIDE LIBRARY®
Your Partner in Crime

YES! Please send me 2 FREE novels from the Worldwide Library™ series and my 2 FREE gifts (gifts are worth about $10). After receiving them, if I don't wish to receive any more books, I can return the shipping statement marked "cancel." If I don't cancel, I will receive 4 brand-new novels every month and be billed just $4.99 per book in the U.S. or $5.99 per book in Canada. That's a saving of 17% off the cover price. It's quite a bargain! Shipping and handling is just 50¢ per book.* I understand that accepting the 2 free books and gifts places me under no obligation to buy anything. I can always return a shipment and cancel at any time. Even if I never buy another book, the two free books and gifts are mine to keep forever.

414/424 WDN E9NE

Name _____ (PLEASE PRINT)

Address _____ Apt. #

City _____ State/Prov. _____ Zip/Postal Code

Signature (if under 18, a parent or guardian must sign)

Mail to **The Reader Service:**
IN U.S.A.: P.O. Box 1867, Buffalo, NY 14240-1867
IN CANADA: P.O. Box 609, Fort Erie, Ontario L2A 5X3

Not valid for current subscribers to the Worldwide Library series.

Want to try two free books from another line?
Call 1-800-873-8635 or visit www.ReaderService.com.

* Terms and prices subject to change without notice. Prices do not include applicable taxes. N.Y. residents add applicable sales tax. Canadian residents will be charged applicable provincial taxes and GST. Offer not valid in Quebec. This offer is limited to one order per household. All orders subject to approval. Credit or debit balances in a customer's account(s) may be offset by any other outstanding balance owed by or to the customer. Please allow 4 to 6 weeks for delivery. Offer available while quantities last.

Your Privacy: Worldwide Library is committed to protecting your privacy. Our Privacy Policy is available online at www.ReaderService.com or upon request from the Reader Service. From time to time we make our lists of customers available to reputable third parties who may have a product or service of interest to you. If you would prefer we not share your name and address, please check here. ☐

Help us get it right—We strive for accurate, respectful and relevant communications. To clarify or modify your communication preferences, visit us at www.ReaderService.com/consumerschoice.

WWLI0